Storm Glass

Storm Glass

JANE URQUHART

The Porcupine's Quill, Inc.

CANADIAN CATALOGUING IN PUBLICATION DATA

Urquhart, Jane, 1949-
  Storm glass

ISBN 0-88984-106-3

I. Title.

PS8591.R68S86 1987   C813'.54   C87-006115-1
PR9199.3.U766S86 1987

Published by the Porcupine's Quill, Inc., 68 Main Street,
Erin, Ontario NOB ITO with financial assistance from
The Canada Council and the Ontario Arts Council.

Some of these stories have previously appeared in
Canadian Fiction Magazine, *Descant* and *The Malahat Review*;
and in the anthologies *Illusions* (Aya Press), *Views from the
North* (Porcupine's Quill) and *Best Canadian Stories* '86
(Oberon Press).

Edited for the press by Doris Cowan.

The front cover is after a photograph by Tony Urquhart,
as are the interior drawings.

Sixth printing, October 1995.

Contents

This book is for Tony

Preface

A CLEAR, PRECISE, WHITE and deadly cold January day is, per-haps, the most uniquely northern and beautiful statement our geography has to offer. On such a day I have finished rereading this collection of stories, most of which, with a couple of exceptions, are about other places.

It seems to me now that the word 'other' is important in that it was an attraction to the mysterious 'other' that started me writing short fiction in the first place: that wild desire to explain, if only to myself, a landscape, an era, a human being, an event, about which I had little knowledge and to which I had but limited access.

Hence, from *Five Wheelchairs,* which I wrote eight years ago and which was my first attempt at fiction of any kind, through *The Death of Robert Browning,* which was composed as a Pro-logue and Epilogue to a novel, to a more recent story such as *Italian Postcards* I have leapt without so much as a 'by your leave' from voice to voice, period to period, gender to gender, landscape to landscape. Writing fiction can be, you see, the most satisfying form of armchair travel.

When I was a child I used to believe that I wanted to be an actress so that I would not be forced to live out my life within the monotonous predictability of a single personality. I'm glad I chose escape writing instead – that journey to the kingdom of 'other' – where the props and the scenery, the players and the games are all under my command. And as I look out my win-dow to the white of the field, the diagonals of the rail fence and the horizontals of the winter trees, I'm grateful, also, that my armchair is situated where it is.

Jane Urquhart
Wellesley, Ontario, January 1987

Five Wheelchairs

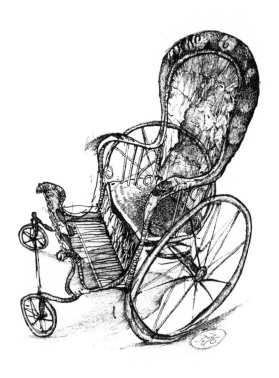

Shoes

LATER THAT EVENING he took off his shoes. He tossed them casually under the grand piano and began dancing. Although he began dancing, he did not stop drinking. He was capable of balancing a full glass of wine on his forehead. He did that now; balancing and drinking, balancing and drinking. The removal of the shoes helped him with the balancing. It also helped him with the dancing. He didn't need any help with the drinking.

The carpet was a soft grey colour and was made of pure wool. Wine from unbalanced glasses had formed permanent purple stains on its surface. But they were mementoes of another time, before he had become polished, practised, professional; before he had learned all there was to know about balance and before he had learned the little that he knew about dancing. He hadn't spilled a drop for months now, except into his open mouth. What was more, he had become able, by a simple bending of the knees, to refill his glass without removing it from his forehead. A master indeed!

She watched him, with some embarrassment, from her wheelchair in the corner. She thought he looked ridiculous, then she thought he looked charming, then she thought he looked ridiculous again. She wondered if balancing acts like this were part of the awesome responsibility one assumed when one was able to move about of one's own accord; that is to say, without the chair. She thought of balancing her teacup on her own forehead but realized that dancing was a necessary, and for her impossible, part of the routine.

Ah, but he was charming dancing there in her living room, moving precariously from step to step like a Niagara daredevil. But oh, there was such tension when he lurched forward or backward in order to prevent a tumble or spill. After a full evening of it she would be exhausted for days; lacking the strength to play show tunes on her piano, lacking the strength to whistle. In fact, she dreaded these performances, which caused her emotions to swing wildly from pleasure to tension and back again. And yet she was somehow addicted and, perhaps because she felt inwardly that no home should be without one, he danced for her often. And balanced too.

Although his neck was beginning to ache, he moved cautiously across the room to the shelf where the records were kept. The third album on the left towards the bottom was the original cast recording of *Annie Get Your Gun*. He admitted the music was dated and silly but he liked it none the less. There was, after all, no business like show business. He was living proof of that. He executed an awkward pirouette, took a healthy swallow of wine, and felt for the record like a blind man reading Braille. He fumbled with the cover and then with the machine. A few minutes later he was moving his arms in time to the tune as if to imitate enthusiastic singing. He did not remove the glass from his forehead.

She was beginning to find the sight of his Adam's apple a bit disconcerting, but positioned as she was, in a room with staircases at every possible exit, she was unable to remove herself from the somewhat uncomfortable scene. She wondered if turning her wheelchair to face the wall would be interpreted as a violent gesture. She decided that, at the very least, it would appear discourteous. She began instead to sing halfheartedly along with the song. 'Your favourite uncle died at dawn,' she sang quietly. 'Top of that your Ma and Pa have parted / you're broken-hearted / but you go on,' she continued. And as she continued his acrobatics seemed charming again, even the lurches. Such is the mysterious power of even the mildest form of participation.

He thought about the ceiling. When he was balancing it filled the entire sphere of his peripheral vision. The ceiling, he decided, was to him now what the floor had been at dancing school; the floor where he had watched his shoes collide with the patent leather attached to the feet of the girls in the class. They who were so much more graceful than he, they who were so much taller. From then on he attributed most of his problems with women to an inability to keep his feet in places where patent leather wasn't. It had soured every relationship and chipped away at his confidence until he had avoided dancing girls altogether. And then one day he had discovered the lady in the wheelchair, and slowly he had begun to dance again, and not only to dance but to balance.

She thought about the hospital and how there was no music there; just the public address system constantly uttering the monotonous names of doctors. There weren't any balancers either. Not unless you took into consideration those few unsteady individuals who had recently been released from crutches. They had practised a kind of delicate, fumbling dance, as if their very bodies were as fragile as the glass this man carried on his forehead. They should have had some music, she concluded in retrospect, while listening to the tune of her own vocal cords increase in volume.

He began to hear her song above the strings and trumpets of the recording. It sounded small and feeble, but it was there none the less. My goodness, she knows the words, he thought as he performed another lurching pirouette. He bent his knees beside the table, refilled his glass, quickly drank the contents, and filled it again. 'There's no people like show people,' he heard her warble in a voice that seemed to be getting stronger and then, 'they smile when they are low.' He cracked his knuckles once or twice to show her that balancing wasn't the only thing that he did well.

By now there was no doubt in her mind that she liked the song. There was also no doubt in her mind that she liked singing the song. Even his Adam's apple was no longer an unpleasant sight when she was singing. In fact, it began to resemble the cheerful bouncing ball of a sing-along film. 'Even with a turkey that you know will fold, you might be stranded out in the cold,' she sang with great vitality. As her mind discovered rhythm her hands beat time on the leather armrests of her wheelchair. She moved everything she could; her mouth, her forehead, her shoulders, her eyebrows, her arms, her stomach. She thought it was a shame that she couldn't tap her patent leather shoes. Just after she had shouted 'next day on your dressing room they've hung a star' and was about to bellow 'let's go on with the show,' his glass fell to the floor.

THE NEXT MORNING he was gone. This was no surprise to her. He was always gone the next morning. Gone, gone, gone. She counted the stains on her one-hundred-percent-wool rug ...

ten ... no, eleven now. The most recent pool was a deeper, richer crimson than the rest, not having had the benefit of time to soften it. She was unable to understand why he had wept when his glass tumbled to the floor the previous evening. Surely not out of consideration for the carpet. Composition-ally, in fact, this particular spill was rather well placed and enhanced the general scheme. He'll get over it, she decided. He always did, and as far as she could gather, he always would.

Then she noticed the shoes. He was gone but his shoes were not. They lay, under the piano, where he had so casually tossed them just before he started balancing. You could tell that they had been abandoned. The laces looked tangled, confused, mis-erable. The tongues lolled obscenely like those of hanged men. One shoe lay on its side and looked as injured and pathetic as an animal that has recently been struck by a car. The other sat bolt upright as if listening for its master's voice. How on earth, she wondered, did he ever get home?

Beyond her window lay a fresh, consistent inch of snow. It must have fallen while she was sleeping. It covered the lawns and the sidewalks. It covered the roofs and the roads. Although it was a cloudy day, reflected white light created the illusion of sunshine and brightened the interior of her home. It added a cheerful overtone to the spectacle of the deserted shoes.

His car had made tracks in the snow. The tracks moved out of the driveway, arced briefly, and advanced toward the end of the street. The long scars they made on the white surface of the road allowed bits of the asphalt to show through – indicating that this was not a cold, definite snow, but one that was likely to disappear by mid-afternoon. She thought that, perhaps, its only function was to remind her of the season and to illustrate the fact of the man's departure: the empirical proof of some-thing she had learned long ago through experience. A kind of resignation settled over her spirit.

Then, as she was about to turn from the window to begin her day, something familiar caught her eye. Pressed into the snow, which lay on the pathway leading from her door to her driveway, were two, long, continuous lines. They might have been made by two children riding bicycles side by side in the snow. They might have been made by a sled. They might even have been made by a baby carriage. But she knew, as surely as she had walked across the room to the window, that they had been made, early that morning, by a departing wheelchair.

She pirouetted once on her patent leather shoes. Then she danced joyfully into the kitchen to make her breakfast. Later that day she would skip to the supermarket to buy a spray can filled with rug shampoo. But not until she'd taken his shoes to the Salvation Army.

Dreams

AS MIGHT BE EXPECTED, her wedding-night dreams were both weird and eventful, taking her in and out of countries that she didn't even know existed. She would later attribute these flights of fancy to the after-effects of the food served at the reception. But that night the dreams gave her no time to ponder the reasons for their arrival. They just kept happening, one after another, until the one about the wheelchairs woke her up, shouting.

But not in fear, or at least not from any worry about her safety. She had felt, in fact, during the course of the dream, remarkably detached, as if she had been watching a play in which she had only one line; a line that was spoken from the wings. But when it came time for her to speak that line she was aware, even in the dream, that it came from some other, surer part of her brain, from those same heretofore-unrecognized countries.

'Don't forget your seatbelts! Don't forget your seatbelts!' she cried, waking both John and herself.

'Seatbelts!' he said. 'What seatbelts?'

She confessed her dream. All the men she had known in her relatively short life had been presented to her in series, like credits at the end of a film. They were all in wheelchairs, but such wheelchairs! Suspended on thin strong ropes they gave their occupants the opportunity to swing back and forth against a clear blue sky. The men involved had looked to her like strange trapeze artists or happy preschool children on playground swings. They were having, it appeared, a wonderful time. Then for reasons unknown even to herself, the cautionary business of the seatbelts had grabbed her vocal cords.

Having no personal use for interpretation of any kind John pronounced the dream absurd and therefore boring. She agreed; they laughed and fell easily back to sleep.

The next morning they jogged two miles along the beach. She was always surprised by the response that the sight of a naked pair of male legs awoke in her. It was honest visual pleasure combined with admiration for a supple functioning form bereft of excess. Male excess was distributed elsewhere, in the face, around the middle, but rarely in the legs. They were holy territory, uninhabited by fat cells. They were perfectly fabricated systems designed, perhaps, to carry primitive hunters quietly and swiftly through some complicated forest. Now they carried John across the sand, through the wind, and along the frothy edges of the sea. Later, in the city, they would carry him through the labyrinth of street and subway to an office every weekday for the rest of his life. She watched the large muscle at the back of his thigh flex and relax with the rhythm of running.

Over lunch, which was served on the terrace of the hotel, they discussed the gifts they had received and divided them into three categories: lovely, passable, and impossible. Yellow was her favourite colour, so all of the yellow paraphernalia slipped easily into the 'lovely' category. The steadily increasing profusion of yellow objects had been, in fact, a great comfort to her in the week or so preceding the wedding. She imagined the one-bedroom apartment they had chosen filling up with radiant sunlight like the gold-leaf backgrounds she had seen in old paintings. She pictured herself bent over a sewing machine stitching yellow gingham curtains while stew bubbled in the yellow enamel pot on the stove. There was also in this picture an image of John, threading his way through the subway system, coming home, on his long lithe legs, to her. At night, she imagined, they would rub themselves all over with the gift of giant yellow bath towels, just before they slipped between the gift of flowered yellow stay-press sheets.

She thought of John's legs rising without a ripple from the yellow bath mat at his feet.

In the category of 'impossible' they placed such items as Blue Mountain pottery and salt and pepper shakers with the words *salty* and *peppy* burned into them.

In 'passable' they placed such items as electric frying pans and waffle irons.

This kind of classification game was one they played often. It had the twofold positive effect of supplying them with conversational material and providing them with a well-ordered private universe. Where categories were concerned they agreed on everything: from music to cocktails, from politics to comic strips, from airports to laundromats. Their value systems were as assured and as tidy as the Holiday Inn at which they were staying. It was all very comforting.

Games notwithstanding, they were neither of them children. He had practised law for a full five years and had, just recently, been offered a partnership in the firm. In his usual practical, deliberate way he had waited a week or so before saying yes to to the proposition. It was the same week that she had handed in her resignation to the paper, giving marriage as her excuse. She felt little regret at the prospect of abandoning her career. Although it had been the job she wanted, the job she had studied for, it had quickly passed through a phase of novelty and into the hazy realm of habit – like most of her affairs. A few days before she left, the girls in the office held a small shower for her. A lot of the accumulated yellow objects were a result of this event.

A combination of the beer they had consumed with lunch and their first morning of strong sunshine had made them feel sleepy. They decided to return to the room for a rest. The desk clerk smiled benignly as they passed through the lobby, his face altering to the odd grimace of a man barely able to suppress a wink. He was aware of their honeymoon status. She remembered passing through similar lobbies of similar hotels with men she had not been married to. The desk clerks there had remained tactfully aloof, the situation being less easy to classify.

After they made love John rolled over and lit a cigarette. Some of the smoke became trapped in the few beams of sun that had managed to penetrate the heavy curtains.

'Why wheelchairs?' he asked. 'Why were they in wheelchairs?'

'Who?' she replied drowsily from the other side of the bed.

'Your boyfriends, your boyfriends in the dream.'

'Who knows?' she said, falling asleep. 'Who ever knows in dreams?'

Later in the afternoon, when they awakened from their nap, John would decide to go for a swim. She would decide to sit on the balcony and write thank-you notes to her friends, the generous donors of 'the lovely, the passable, and the impossible'. 'Dear Lillian,' she would begin. Then something would capture her attention. It would be the sight of John walking down across the beach towards the water, walking on his beautiful spare legs. With his back turned he would be unaware that she was watching him. He would become smaller and smaller until, at last, he would collapse into the water. She would study the predictable repetitious motions of the waves surrounding him until, with a kind of slow horror, she would realize that the organized behaviour of the Atlantic was what the rest of her life would be, one week following another, expectations fulfilled in easy categories, and the hypnotic monotony of predictable responses. Oh, my God, she would think briefly – why does he seem to be having such a good time?

Then she would dismiss this and all other related thoughts from her mind forever and continue her thank-you note.

'Dear Lillian,' she would write, 'John and I just love Blue Mountain pottery.'

Charity

WHEN SHE ARRIVED at the hospital they put her in a wheel-chair. Under the circumstances this seemed somewhat absurd. Certainly there was something wrong with her. Yes, something was definitely wrong with her. But nothing, as far as she knew, was wrong with her legs. At least not yet. But then she remembered. In hospitals they always put you in a wheelchair. Regardless of what the problem was, if you could still sit up they put you in a wheelchair. Probably to assure you that you were sick, even if you weren't.

But she was sick. Just that morning she had announced to him, between sobs, 'Harold, I'm sick,' and then, when he didn't respond, 'I'm *sick,* Harold. Put me in the hospital!'

After that he had sighed, put down the newspaper, and walked across the room to the telephone. She had continued to sob, her face buried in her hands, but she had left a tiny crack between her fingers so that she could see what he was doing. He was fumbling through his address book looking for the phone number of the doctor.

'God, he's slow!' she mumbled to no one in particular.

Eventually, and on the kindly advice of the family physician, he had taken her to the hospital. But let it be noted that he took his sweet time about it. It seemed to her that they had driven around each block six times before advancing to the next. She was probably right. He often played little tricks like this when he was taking her to the hospital. He hated taking her to the hospital. He thought it was ridiculous. She was perfectly aware of his feelings but she was also aware that they got there none the less. So there she sat in the wheelchair and there he stood at the admitting desk yawning over the same old tedious forms. She gathered together all the loathing she could muster and aimed it at the indentation just beneath his skull and in the centre of his shaved neck. To her amusement he brought his left hand up and scratched that very spot, just as he might have had an insect landed there.

She didn't like him much and that was the truth. He didn't

like her much either, but then, what did he like? Certainly not his job at the Kleaning Cloth factory, which was boring and repetitious; certainly not his children who had, mercifully, all grown up and moved away; certainly not his dog who bit him daily, on his departure for and his arrival from the Kleaning Cloth factory, and certainly not these idiotic forms he had to fill out every single time he brought her to the hospital. He also didn't like the itchy feeling he got at the base of his neck each time he turned his back in her presence. The terrible truth about all these things was that they were, in his eyes, ridiculous as well. Not only was she ridiculous but everything connected to her was ridiculous: her tears were ridiculous, her meals were ridiculous, and whatever the hell was wrong with her was ridiculous. Her ridiculous doctors, in their ridiculous, kindly wisdom, could not bring themselves to tell him what was, in fact, wrong with her. Finally he stopped asking, and the minute he stopped asking he stopped caring.

Her suitcase, he knew, was filled with ridiculous negligées, which she had ordered, over the years, from the back sections of movie magazines and comic books kept especially for her hospital experiences. He handed this precious cargo to a nurse who had appeared, like a long-awaited taxi, around the corner. Then he turned to leave. Just as he was about to enter the revolving glass doors he heard the nurse chirp to his wife, 'And how are we today?' He thought this was a ridiculous question to ask anyone who sat sobbing in a wheelchair.

WHEN SHE WAS CERTAIN that he had gone she stopped sobbing. Soon she was gliding through green halls, in and out of elevators, past rooms filled with fragrant flowers. She looked forward, with great pleasure, to her lunch which she knew would arrive on silent rubber wheels and would include fluorescent pink Jello topped with Dream Whip. Once in her room she picked out a fluorescent pink negligée to wear, knowing that it would match the Jello. Then she slipped between the delicious, starched white sheets and relaxed against the smooth, firm fibre of the hospital mattress. Let the bastard pack his own Twinkies, she said to herself just before she fell into a deep and dreamless sleep.

She awoke an hour later to the arrival of her anticipated lunch. It was everything that she had hoped and she devoured it with relish, right down to the last, tiny, quivering mouthful. Then she reached into the night table drawer for the two wonderful books that she had stuffed into her suitcase along with the negligées. One of these books was entitled *Lovelier After Forty* and the other *How to Develop Your Personality, A New You!* Both had been written by an ex-heavyweight champion with whom she was, of course, in love. She could never hope to meet him but she was in love with him anyway. Contact was incidental. It was the tone of his words that attracted her. They were easy words; words that made her feel warm and comfortable in a way that Harold never had. During her frequent stays at the hospital she would often spend her afternoons imagining 'the champion' (as she secretly called him) bending over her like a parasol of rippling muscles and shining skin, breathing easy words into her ears.

'Many a homely younger woman has, through persistence, turned herself into a beautiful, lovable, older woman,' he would whisper, and then, 'You are not alone. There *are* order and truth and eternal reality in the universe.'

And when she danced with him upon the shores of her imagination he crooned exotic instructions into the microphone of her brain.

'Draw hips slightly forward then flick backwards quickly as if to strike imaginary wall with buttocks ...,' he would sigh. Then she would sigh and chant along with his ballroom litanies, while her stark, private room turned from institution to palace, to mysterious night club, to the starlight lounge, to Hernando's Hideaway.

During this particular stay at the hospital, dancing took up some of her time but the greatest portion of her energy was devoted to personal development; that is, the development of her NEW SELF, a self that would necessarily be lovelier after forty. There were, she knew, seven success secrets and the champion had assured her that the mastery of these would result in a young and magnetic personality. SECFIMP was the key, seven was the number:

1   S   Sincerity
2   E   Enthusiasm
3   C   Charity
4   F   Friendliness
5   I   Initiative
6   M   Memory
7   P   Persistence

And the greatest of these was charity.

HOW KIND SHE WAS to the champion, sewing imaginary buttons on his skin-tight clothing and cooking up imaginary feasts in her brain. She allowed him to read newspapers or watch ball games all night and she never complained. She ironed his imaginary socks. She kept his imaginary house spotlessly clean and she never burdened him with her own insignificant problems. She showed a definite interest in his career, encouraging him to confess to her those tiny nagging moments of self-doubt that afflict every man at one stage or another. But most importantly, she wore her negligées constantly in an effort to keep herself as young and attractive as she was the day she first imagined him.

He was pleased but not entirely satisfied. He introduced her to his greatest beauty secret – a three-week plan to beautify her bust contour. He assured her that no one was more interested in helping her with this delicate problem than he. He sympathized. He understood. Hadn't he once been a ninety-pound weakling, who through persistent effort had raised himself to the very heights of power and personal magnetism? Hadn't he counselled countless other women who were suffering from the misery and self-consciousness of possessing an unattractive bosom? Didn't he know everything there was to know about the growth and tone of pectoral muscles? Of course he did. Of course he had. And he would help her by setting out a rigid schedule of exercises that she could begin that very day.

The weeks rolled by both in illusion and in reality. Nurses glided in and out of her makeshift gym. They trod softly on squeaky shoes. They carried their trays of Jello and Dream

Whip with courtly precision. They wrote mysterious messages on the chart at the foot of her bed. They gathered in huddles and murmured outside her door. They brought in fresh white slabs of clean starched sheets. They distributed pills and tiny paper cups filled with lukewarm water. They administered enemas. Their wedding bands glowed on their smooth white hands. And they tactfully ignored the presence of the champion, to all intents and purposes didn't see him at all. And so, of course, they couldn't notice how, when the wheelchair, which would take their patient back to the lobby where Harold was waiting, appeared at the door, a man in skin-tight clothing put down his barbells and scratched the back of his neck, just as he might have had an insect landed there.

Gift

MONSIEUR DELACOUR was certain that it was spring. 'Spring is here,' he announced, silently, to himself. The thought rattled in the rafters of his brain, avoiding altogether the area phrenologists label *voice*. Monsieur Delacour hadn't had a voice for years. Some mysterious being or event had snatched it away from him and, the truth was, Monsieur Delacour couldn't have cared less.

He also didn't care about his left side. Whoever or whatever had snatched away the voice part of his brain had also made off with the area that controls the left arm and leg. And so Monsieur Delacour got around with the aid of a wooden crutch and his wonderful talent for hopping. A long, thin man, who had always resembled a large wading bird, Monsieur Delacour had adjusted, years ago, to his one-legged method of transportation. It suited him just fine. Later a doctor would actually remove the non-functioning left leg. But, at the moment, it was still attached to Monsieur Delacour. Still, he didn't care about it. Not one bit.

He did, however, care about spring, and now, despite the winter chill that still hung in the air, he knew it was spring. His stubborn belief was based on the fact that today, for the first time in six months, a tiny feeble ray of sun had entered the damp octagonal square where Monsieur Delacour's house occupied a corner. The sunbeam had paused briefly on a mouldy stone wall and then had quickly disappeared as if it were in a hurry to visit more attractive places; where grasses, or even weeds, were conceivable.

But sun, you say, can enter enclosed spaces even in winter. Not these spaces, not those winters. The sun had barely the strength to drag itself above the horizon, never mind the bravery to invade the narrow twisting streets and the slimy paved piazzas of Monsieur Delacour's home town. Tall mossy walls everywhere, grey-green vegetation of the parasitic variety, everyone relocated or dead of the plague in the year 1527; that's what it was like. We tourists love places like this. We think they look like the environments of fairy tales. We have never lived there.

But Monsieur Delacour loved it too – because it was his home town and because it provided him with a corner in which to live. Here he did what he could with his chickens and rabbits, did what he could with his wife. It had become apparent, early in his relationship with her, that whoever or whatever had snatched away the parts of his brain labelled *voice, left arm,* and *left leg,* had decided to leave the area marked *privates* totally unaltered. Hence Monsieur Delacour could do a great deal with his wife. And at the moment that we find him watching the sun on the wall he had eight children. And there would be more.

Monsieur Delacour's wife was a handful. 'She's a handful,' said Monsieur Delacour, silently. Then he chuckled to himself. Like everything else the chuckle rattled in the rafters of his brain, refused, as it was, the release of vocal cords. A large woman, whose remaining teeth had been seriously eroded by the constant assault of chocolate, Madame Delacour was interested in everything: from weather to underwear, from school to defecation, from witches to astronauts, from politics to wheelchairs. And she would talk to anyone; to you or me or dogs or cats or chickens or the mayor or the curé. It was all the same to her.

It was winter that made her a handful. In a town where nothing happens in the summer, less than nothing happens in the winter and Madame Delacour became bored. Nothing helped: not the television, which by virtue of its size blocked the only window in the house; not the kids, whose collective naughty imagination would keep the most blasé among us on our toes; not the constant supply of chocolate which was made possible by cheques from the state that arrived at the door. Winter bored her, absolutely and completely, and nothing helped. Nothing that is, except death.

Madame Delacour was fervently drawn to the drama and ceremony of death. Not her own, of course. That was, as she wisely knew, a party she could not attend. But anyone else's fascinated her. She appeared at all the funerals she could, dressed appropriately for the occasion in her vast purple dress and with lipstick smeared all over her wide mouth and sparse teeth. She mourned with the mourners and eulogized with the eulogizers. Often her sadness was sincere, but more often the excitement that death causes in a small town cancelled all but the most fleeting of sorrows. Madame Delacour at a funeral was like a child at a birthday party, and the corpse like a brand new, recently unwrapped gift.

But there was a small problem. There were simply not enough deaths to keep her occupied. The tiny population of the town could only produce a certain number each year, and although most of these occurred, conveniently, in the darkest and most boring part of the winter, Madame Delacour became restless and dissatisfied. Boredom waited for her on the street after each funeral. She began to invent deaths.

And so it came to be that, after a few long dark winters, almost everyone in the town had been reported dead three or four times before they, in fact, expired. Madame Delacour became, as Monsieur Delacour so aptly and so silently put it, a handful. Even the dogs and the chickens avoided her chatter. Everyone likes to discuss the actual death of a neighbour, but invented death is something else. It's foolish to weep and bemoan the fate of a friend who, at that very moment, is buying two tins of pâté and a grosse baguette in the local épicerie. And it's most embarrassing if and when the friend in question finds out about your outburst of emotion. And so, as Madame Delacour found fewer and fewer people with whom to discuss imaginary death she turned more and more to her husband.

Monsieur Delacour loved his wife. And it wasn't that he was against death either. He just didn't care about it one bit. Someone or something could come and snatch it away for all the difference it would make to him. He was far more interested in the children, chickens and rabbits who all fitted nicely, if a little snugly, into his small corner in the square. He liked to watch their numbers increase. It was something he could count on. He wished his wife had something she could count on too, for Monsieur Delacour was as certain as could be that all of the important deaths had already happened.

Because he could not speak, Monsieur Delacour's thoughts consisted mostly of observations and explanations, which he put to himself in the form of announcements. Questions were, you might say, out of the question since they could not be articulated. And only occasionally did he make decisions; only when it was absolutely necessary. He felt it was necessary now.

'Spring is here,' he announced, silently, to himself. 'In spring Madame Delacour visits the larger square near the church and watches the tourists come and go. Then she makes up stories about the people she has seen there; movie stars and counts and earls, thieves and convicted murderers, millionaires and soccer players, queens and presidents all stream into her imagination and the power of death subsides. She will be perfectly happy watching this parade of strangers that lasts through the summer and on into the fall. But then the fanciful funerals will begin again. Something has to be done about her.'

And, oddly enough, just that morning Social Services had decided that they must do something about Monsieur Delacour. Around nine o'clock a plump, cheerful man had leapt out of a white van. Then he had dragged a brand new wheelchair into Monsieur Delacour's kitchen. He had sat in it himself in order to demonstrate its safety and efficiency. He had shown Monsieur Delacour how to work the gears and manipulate the wheels. It had shone in the grimy kitchen as brightly as a diamond tiara. It was like a carriage for a king. And Monsieur Delacour didn't care about it at all. It seemed to him to be just one more contraption that might be snatched away at any moment. So, as soon as the white van had pulled away, Monsieur Delacour hopped outside to his stone bench in order to watch for spring.

It was the combination of the change of the season and the appearance of the wheelchair that gave him the idea and that brought about the decision. He would give Madame Delacour the wheelchair for the winter. He didn't, after all, care about it one bit and, unlike the use of his voice, left arm and left leg, he could be sure that he had donated it to a worthy cause. With a little goat's bell attached to it, and a colourful cushion placed in the seat, it would be the perfect vehicle for her imagination. She could spend the winter months inventing the illnesses that had forced her into the chair; illnesses that were awe-inspiring but not fatal – a party she could attend. She would turn her attention away from other people's deaths and towards her own diseases.

Monsieur Delacour leaned back against the cold stone wall behind him. Anticipation rattled happily through his brain. First he anticipated the summer afternoons when the sun would warm (though never dry) the stones around his corner. Then he anticipated the seven pink petunias Madame Delacour could place in a box outside the single window that the television blocked. Then he thought about his own death, which he didn't care about in the least, but which would be the greatest of his gifts to Madame Delacour. And finally, with a definite smile, he thought about Madame Delacour, herself, and how she would look in her winter wheelchair, moving through the streets of town, accompanied by the distant voice of a tiny bell. Freed from the clutches of boredom her face, he decided, would reflect a combination of invented pain and immeasurable happiness.

The Drawing Master

ALL BUT ONE of his students were drawing the canopied bed. Eleven of them were fixed, with furious attention, on the object, puzzling out the perspective and gritting their teeth over the intricate folds provided by the drapery of its rather dirty velvet curtains. Pencils in hand they twitched, scratched heads, scratched paper and erased. Individually, each studied his neighbour's work and vowed to give up drawing altogether. Collectively, they laboured with a singleness of purpose worthy of great frescoed ceilings and large blocks of marble. All for the rendering of a rather tatty piece of furniture where someone, long forgotten, had no doubt slept and maybe died.

He walked silently behind the group, noting how the object shrank, swelled, attained monumentality, or became deformed from notebook to notebook. What, he wondered, brought them to this? In a building full of displayed objects, why this automatic attraction to the funereal cast of velvet and dark wood? This must be the bed that the child in all of them longed to possess; to draw the dusty curtains round and suffocate in magic of contained privacy. It would be as cosy and frilly and mysterious as the darkened spaces underneath the fabric of their mother's skirts. The womb, he concluded, moves them like a magnet in all or any of its symbolic disguises.

The twelfth of the bunch was drawing a stuffed bird. Mottled by time and distorted by the glass bell that covered it, it pretended, without much credibility, to be singing its heart out perched on a dry twig. Its former colours, whatever they might have been, were now reduced to something approaching grey. The face of the young man who had chosen to reproduce this bundle of feathers was reflected once in the glass bell and again in the display case, and was also greyish. The drawing master glanced quickly over the young man's shoulder and discovered, as he had expected, a great deal of nothing. Fifteen years in the profession had taught him to read all signs with cynicism. A student who kept aloof from the crowd, or chose alternate subject matter: these, to his mind, were social rather than creative decisions.

'You must like birds, Roger,' he commented wryly, and then, 'There are some who seem to prefer beds.'

The young man's face acquired a spot of colour, but in no other way did he respond to the remark.

The drawing master moved on. At this point there was little he could do for them except leave them alone. This was usually the case once he had taught them the rules: he believed, through it all, that the rules were the bones of the work. Within the structure they provided, great experiments could be performed, giant steps could be taken. And so his students suffered through weeks of colour theory, months of perspective. They reduced great painting to the geometry of compositional analysis. Like kindergarten children, they arranged triangles and squares on construction paper. Then, after a written test, in which the acquired basics were transposed to paper, he hired a small bus and drove them to this old, provincial museum, where he allowed them to choose their own subject matter. Year after year, the drawing master searched in vain for the student who would make the giant step, who would perform the great experiment, just as year after year he looked for evidence of the same experiment, the same step, in his own work.

The drawing master moved on and now he was looking for his own subject matter. For he had brought with him a small bottle of ink and a tin box in which he kept his straight pen and his nibs. He could feel this paltry equipment weighing down his right-hand pocket, altering somewhat the drape of his jacket. Aware of this, he often rearranged the tools giving himself the look of a man with an abundance of coins that he like to jingle. Then he shifted his shoulders back and mentally convinced himself that a slight bulge at the hip could not alter a look of dignity so long in the making. There were still, after all, the faultless cravat, the leather pants, and the well-trimmed beard speckled with grey.

And now he began to move past display cases; one filled with butter presses, another with spinning wheels, still another containing miniature interiors of pioneer dwellings, complete with tiny hooked rugs and patchwork quilts. He paused briefly before the collection of early Canadian cruets, interested in the delicate lines of twisted silver. But they turned to drawings so quickly in his mind that the actual execution on paper seemed futile and boring and he walked away from them. Past blacksmith's tools and tomahawks, past moccasins and arrowheads and beadwork, past churns and depressed glass, past century-old pottery from Quebec and early models of long-silent telephones, past ridiculously modern mannequins clothed in the nineteenth century, until he found himself looking through the glass of a window and out into the fields.

And then he thought of the drive through the countryside to this small county museum, which had been situated, with the intention of pleasing both, between the two major towns of the surrounding vicinity. The students, nervous and silent in such close quarters with their teacher, had offered little interference to the flow of his consciousness and he had almost become absorbed by the rush of the landscape as it flashed past the windows of the van. A strong wind had confused the angle of fields of tall grass and had set the normally well-organized trees lurching against the sky. Laundry had become desperate splashes of colour in farm-yards. Even the predictable black-and-white of docile cows seemed temporary, as if they might be sent spiralling towards fence wire like so much tumbleweed. The restlessness of this insistent motion, this constant churning hyperactivity, had distracted the drawing master, but he had felt the strong, hard-edged responsibility of the highway to such an extent that even now, when he observed the landscape through the safe, confining frame of the window, he was somehow unable to grasp it. And he turned back towards the interior of the museum.

Here he sketched, for his own amusement and possibly for the amusement of his children at home, two or three elderly puppets that hung dejectedly from strings attached to flat wooden crosses. Completing, with a few well-executed strokes, the moronic wide-eyed stare of the last one, he cleaned the nib of his pen with a rag that he carried with him for that purpose, and prepared to return to his class. Then his eye was caught by a large white partition set back against the left-hand corner of the room. He walked over to it with a kind of idle curiosity and peered around its edge.

There, awaiting either repair or display case, and hopelessly stacked together like tumbling hydro towers, were five Victorian wicker wheelchairs. A few had lost, either through overuse or neglect, the acceptable curve of their shape and sagged over their wheels like fat women. One had retained its shape but the woven grid of its back was interrupted by large gaping holes. The small front wheels of another had become permanently locked into a pigeon-toed position through decades of lack of oil. All in all they appeared to be at least as crippled as their absent occupants must have been – as if by some magic process each individual's handicap had been mysteriously transferred to his chair. The drawing master was fascinated. He had found his subject matter.

An hour later he had completed five small drawings. They were, as he knew, his best. The crazy twisted personality of each chair distributed itself with ease across the surface of the paper. Expressed in his fine line their abandoned condition became wistfully personal, as sad as forsaken toys in the attic or tricycles in the basement, childless for years. Vacant coffins, open graves, funeral wreaths – they were all there, competing with go-carts and red wagons. The drawing master carefully placed his precious drawings in his jacket pocket. When he arrived home that evening he would mat and frame them and put them under glass. But now he would stroll casually over to his pupils, who had dispersed and were wandering around the room gazing absently into display cases.

Except for the one young man who seemed still to be involved in the rendering of the dead bird. The drawing master approached him and bent over his shoulder to offer his usual words of quiet criticism – perhaps a few words about light and shade, or something about texture. He drew back, however, astonished. There before him on the paper was a perfectly drawn skeleton of a bird, and surrounding that and sometimes covering it or being covered by it, in a kind of crazy spatial ambiguity, drawn in by the student with the blunt ends of a pocketful of crayons, was the mad, turbulent landscape. It shuddered and heaved and appeared to be germinating from the motionless structure of the bird whose bones the young man had sensed beneath dust and feathers. It needed no glass to protect it, no frame to confine it. And it was as confused and disordered and wonderful as everything the drawing master had chosen to ignore.

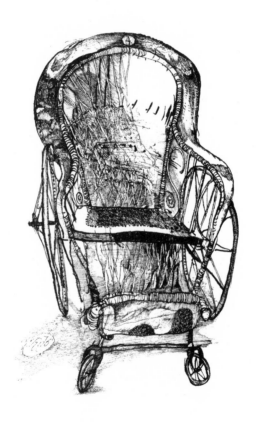

Storm Glass

FROM WHERE SHE LAY she could see the lake. It seemed to her to be heading east, as if it had a definite destination in mind and would someday be gone altogether from the place where it was now. But it was going nowhere; though diminished by sun, replenished by rain and pushed around by strong winds, it was always a lake. And always there. God knows it had its twentieth-century problems; its illnesses, its weaknesses. Some had even said it was dying. But she knew better. She was dying, and although she felt as close as a cousin to the lake, she did not sense that it shared with her this strong, this irreversible decline. It would always be a lake, and always there, long after she had gone somewhere else. Alone.

She was alone in the room now. As alone as she would be a few months later when the brightness of the last breath closed on the dark, forever. She had imagined the voyage in that dark – her thoughts speaking in an alien tongue – textural black landscape – non-visual – swimming towards the change. And then she had hoped that she would be blessed with some profound last words, some small amount of theatre to verify the end of things. But somehow she sensed it would be more of a letting go, slipping right through the centre of the concentric circles that are the world and into a private and inarticulate focus, and then ...

The shore had changed again and again since her first summers there. One year there had been unexpected sand for her babies to play in. She remembered fine grains clinging to their soggy diapers, and their flat sturdy footprints which had existed for seconds only before the lake gathered them up. But a storm the following winter had altered the patterns of the water and the next year her small children had staggered over beach stones to the edge. In subsequent weeks their bare feet had toughened, allowing them to run over rocks and pebbles without pain. Her own feet had resisted the beach stones summer after summer, forcing her to wear some kind of shoes until she left the land for the smooth softness of the water.

Her husband, larger, more stubborn, less willing to admit to weaknesses than she, would brave the distance of the beach, like the children, barefoot. But his feet had never toughened, and standing, as she sometimes had, on the screened veranda, she had watched the pain move through his stiffened legs and up his back until, like a large performing animal, he had fallen, backwards and laughing, into the lake.

He was not there now, unwilling to admit to this, her last, most impossible weakness.

Yet he came and went, mostly at mealtimes, when a hired woman came to cook for them. He came in heavy with the smell of the farm where he had worked and worked, making things come to be; a field of corn, a litter of pigs, or even a basket of smooth, brown eggs. The farm took all of his time now, as if, as she moved down this isolated tunnel towards that change, it was even more important that he make things come to be. And though this small summer cottage was only minutes away from the earth that he worked, the fact of her lying there had made it a distance too great for him to travel except for the uncontrollable and predictable necessities of hunger and of sleep.

The beach was smaller this year, and higher. Strong spring winds had urged the lake to push the stones into several banks, like large steps, up to the grass. These elevations curved in a regular way around the shoreline as if a natural amphitheatre had been mysteriously provided so that audiences of pilgrims might come and sit and watch the miracle of the lake. They never arrived, of course, but she sometimes found it fun to conjure the image of the beach filled with spectators, row on row, cheering on the glide of a wave, the leap of a fish, the flash of a white sail on the horizon. In her imagination she could see their backs, an array of colourful shirts, covering the usual solid grey of the stones.

And yet, even without the imaginary spectators, the grey was not entirely solid. Here and there a white stone shone amongst the others, the result of some pre-Cambrian magic. In other years the children had collected these and old honey pails full of them still lined the windowsills on the porch. The children had changed, had left, had disappeared into adulthood, lost to cities and success. And yet they too came and went with smiles and gifts and offers of obscure and indefinite forms of help. She remembered mending things for them; a toy, a scratch on the skin, a piece of clothing, and she understood their helpless, inarticulate desire to pretend that now they could somehow mend her.

In her room there were two windows. One faced the lake, the other the weather, which always seemed to come in from the east. In the mornings when the sun shone, a golden rectangle appeared like an extra blanket placed on the bed by some anonymous benevolent hand. On those days her eyes moved from the small flame of her opal ring to the millions of diamonds scattered on the lake and she wished that she could lie out there among them, rolling slightly with the current until the sun moved to the other side of the sky. During the heat of all those summers she had never strayed far from the water, teaching her children to swim or swimming herself in long graceful strokes, covering the distance from one point of land to another, until she knew by heart the shoreline and the horizon visible from the small bay where the cottage was situated. And many times she had laughed and called until at last, with a certain reluctance, her husband had stumbled over the stones to join her.

He seldom swam now, and if he did it was early in the morning before she was awake. Perhaps he did not wish to illustrate to her his mobility, and her lack of it. Or perhaps, growing older, he wished his battle with the lake to be entirely private. In other times she had laughed at him for his method of attacking the lake, back bent, shoulders drawn forward, like a determined prize fighter, while she slipped effortlessly by, as fluid as the water, and as relaxed. His moments in the lake were tense, and quickly finished; a kind of enforced pleasure, containing more comedy than surrender.

But sometimes lately she had awakened to see him, shivering and bent, scrambling into his overalls in some far corner of the room and knowing he had been swimming, she would ask the customary questions about the lake. 'Was it cold? Was there much of an undertow?' and he had replied with the customary answers. 'Not bad, not really, once you are in, once you are used to it.'

That morning he had left her early, without swimming. The woman had made her bed, bathed her and abandoned her to the warm wind that drifted in one window and the vision of the beach and the lake that occupied the other. Her eyes scanned the stones beyond the glass trying to remember the objects that, in the past, she had found among them. Trying to remember, for instance, the look and then the texture of the clean dry bones of seagulls; more delicate than the dried stems of chrysanthemums and more pleasing to her than that flower in full bloom. These precise working parts of once animate things were so whole in themselves that they left no evidence of the final breakdown of flesh and feather. They were suspended somewhere between being and non-being like the documentation of an important event and their presence somehow justified the absence of all that had gone before.

But then, instead of bone, she caught sight of a minuscule edge of colour, blue-green, a dusty shine, an irregular shape surrounded by rounded rocks – so small she ought not to have seen it, she ought to have overlooked it altogether.

'Storm glass,' she whispered to herself, and then she laughed realizing that she had made use of her husband's words without thinking, without allowing the pause of reason to interrupt her response as it so often did. When they spoke together she sometimes tried expressly to avoid his words, to be in possession of her own, hard thoughts. Those words and thoughts, she believed, were entirely her own. They were among the few things he had no ability to control with either his force or his tenderness.

It must have been at least fifteen summers before, when the children, bored and sullen in the clutches of early adolescence, had sat day after day like ominous boulders on the beach, until she, remembering the honey pails on the windowsills, had suggested that they collect the small pieces of worn glass that were sometimes scattered throughout the stones. Perhaps, she had remarked, they could do something with them; build a small patio or path, or fill glass mason jars to decorate their bedrooms. It would be better, at least, than sitting at the water's edge wondering what to do with the endless summer days that stretched before them.

The three children had begun their search almost immediately; their thin backs brown and shining in the hot sun. Most of the pieces they found were a dark ochre colour, beer bottles no doubt, thrown into the lake by campers from the provincial park fifteen miles down the road. But occasionally they would come across a rarer commodity, a kind of soft turquoise glass similar to the colour of bottles they had seen in antique shops with their mother. These fragments sometimes caused disputes over who had spotted them first but, as often as not, there were enough pieces to go fairly around. Still rarer and smaller were the particles of emerald green and navy blue, to be found among the tiny damp pebbles at the very edge of the shore, the remnants of bottles even more advanced in age than those that were available in the shops. But the children had seen these intact as well, locked behind the glass of display cases in the county museum. Often the word *poison* or a skull and crossbones would be visible in raised relief across the surface of this older, darker glassware. Their mother knew that the bottles had held cleaning fluid, which was as toxic now in its cheerful tin and plastic containers as it had been then housed in dark glass, but the children associated it with dire and passionate plots, perhaps involving pirates, and they held it up to their parents as the most important prize of all.

The combing of the beach had lasted two days, maybe three, and had become, for a while, the topic of family conversations. But one evening, she remembered, when they were all seated at the table, her husband had argued with her, insisting as he often did on his own personal form of definition – even in the realm of the activities of children.

'It's really storm glass,' he had announced to the children who had been calling it by a variety of different names, 'that's what I always called it.'

'But,' she had responded, 'I remember a storm glass from high school, from physics, something to do with predicting weather, I don't know just what. But that's what it is, not the glass out there on the beach.'

'No,' he had continued, 'storms make it with waves and stones. That wears down the edges. You can't take the edge off a piece of glass that lies at the bottom of a bird bath. Storms make it, it's storm glass.'

'Well, we always called it beach glass, or sometimes water glass when we were children, and the storm glass came later when we were in high school.'

'It is storm glass,' he said, with the kind of grave finality she had come to know; a statement you don't retract, a place you don't return from.

It was after these small, really insignificant, disputes that they would turn silently away from each other for a while; she holding fiercely, quietly, to her own privacy, her own person. To him it seemed she refused out of stubbornness to accept his simplified sense of the order of things, that she wished to confuse him by leaning towards the complexities of alternatives. He was not a man of great intellect. Almost every issue that he had questioned had settled into fact and belief in early manhood. He clung to the predictability of these preordained facts with such tenacity that when she became ill the very enormity of the impending disorder frightened him beyond words and into the privacy of his own belief that it was not so, could not be happening to her, or, perhaps more importantly, to him. They did not speak of it but turned instead quietly from each other, she not wishing to defend her own tragedy, and he not wishing to submit to any reference to such monumental change.

But fifteen years before, in the small matter of the glass, the children had submitted easily, as children will, to the sound of his authority; and storm glass it had become. Within a week, however, their project had been abandoned in favour of boredom and neither path nor patio had appeared. Nevertheless, the glass itself appeared year after year among the stones on the beach and, try as she might, she could never quite control the impulse to pick it up. The desire to collect it was with her even now, creating an invisible tension, like a slim, taut wire, from her eyes to her hands to the beach as she lay confined within her room. It was, after all, a small treasure, an enigma; broken glass robbed by time of one of its more important qualities, the ability to cut. And though she could no longer rub it between her palms she knew it would be as firm and as strong as ever. And as gentle.

From where she lay she could see the lake and she knew that this was good; to be able to see the land and the end of the land, to be able to see the vast indefinite bowl of the lake. And she was pleased that she had seen the storm glass. She felt she understood the evolution of its story. What had once been a shattered dangerous substance now lay upon the beach, harmless, inert and beautiful after being tossed and rubbed by the real weather of the world. It had, with time, become a pastel memory of a useful vessel, to be carried, perhaps in a back pocket, and brought out and examined now and then. It was a relic of that special moment when the memory and the edge of the break softened and combined in order to allow preservation.

How long, she wondered, did it take, from the break on the rocks, through the storms of different seasons, to the change? When did the edges cease to cut?

That night he came in tired and heavy, followed by the smell of making things come to be. He spoke of problems with the farm, of obstinate machinery that refused to function or of crops with inexplicable malformations – events that, even in the power of his stubbornness, he could never hope to control. And when he turned to look at her his eyes were like fresh broken glass: sharp, dangerous, alive. She answered him with kindness, though, knowing the storm ahead and then the softening of edges yet to come.

'There's storm glass on the beach,' she said.

The Death of Robert Browning

IN DECEMBER OF 1889, as he was returning by gondola from the general vicinity of the Palazzo Manzoni, it occurred to Robert Browning that he was more than likely going to die soon. This revelation had nothing to do with either his advanced years or the state of his health. He was seventy-seven, a reasonably advanced age, but his physical condition was described by most of his acquaintances as vigorous and robust. He took a cold bath each morning and every afternoon insisted on a three-mile walk during which he performed small errands from a list his sister had made earlier in the day. He drank moderately and ate well. His mind was as quick and alert as ever.

Nevertheless, he knew he was going to die. He also had to admit that the idea had been with him for some time – two or three months at least. He was not a man to ignore symbols, especially when they carried personal messages. Now he had to acknowledge that the symbols were in the air as surely as winter. Perhaps, he speculated, a man carried the seeds of his death with him always, somewhere buried in his brain, like the face of a woman he is going to love. He leaned to one side, looked into the deep waters of the canal, and saw his own face reflected there. As broad and distinguished and cheerful as ever, health shining vigorously, robustly from his eyes – even in such a dark mirror.

Empty Gothic and Renaissance palaces floated on either side of him like soiled pink dreams. Like sunsets with dirty faces, he mused, and then, pleased with the phrase, he reached into his jacket for his notebook, ink pot and pen. He had trouble recording the words, however, as the chill in the air had numbed his hands. Even the ink seemed affected by the cold, not flowing as smoothly as usual. He wrote slowly and deliberately, making sure to add the exact time and the location. Then he closed the book and returned it with the pen and pot to his pocket, where he curled and uncurled his right hand for some minutes until he felt the circulation return to normal. The celebrated Venetian dampness was much worse in winter, and

Browning began to look forward to the fire at his son's palazzo where they would be beginning to serve afternoon tea, perhaps, for his benefit, laced with rum.

A sudden wind scalloped the surface of the canal. Browning instinctively looked upwards. Some blue patches edged by ragged white clouds, behind them wisps of grey and then the solid dark strip of a storm front moving slowly up on the horizon. Such a disordered sky in this season. No solid, predictable blocks of weather with definite beginnings, definite endings. Every change in the atmosphere seemed an emotional response to something that had gone before. The light, too, harsh and metallic, not at all like the golden Venice of summer. There was something broken about all of it, torn. The sky, for instance, was like a damaged canvas. Pleased again by his own metaphorical thoughts, Browning considered reaching for the notebook. But the cold forced him to reject the idea before it had fully formed in his mind.

Instead, his thoughts moved lazily back to the place they had been when the notion of death so rudely interrupted them; back to the building he had just visited. Palazzo Manzoni. *Bello, bello* Palazzo Manzoni! The colourful marble medallions rolled across Browning's inner eye, detached from their home on the Renaissance façade, and he began, at once, to reconstruct for the thousandth time the imaginary windows and balconies he had planned for the building's restoration. In his daydreams the old poet had walked over the palace's swollen marble floors and slept beneath its frescoed ceilings, lit fires underneath its sculptured mantels and entertained guests by the light of its chandeliers. Surrounded by a small crowd of admirers he had read poetry aloud in the evenings, his voice echoing through the halls. *No R.B. tonight,* he had said to them, winking, *Let's have some real poetry.* Then, moving modestly into the palace's impressive library, he had selected a volume of Dante or Donne.

But they had all discouraged him and it had never come to pass. Some of them said that the façade was seriously cracked and the foundations were far from sound. Others told him that the absentee owner would never part with it for anything resembling a fair price. Eventually, friends and family wore him down with their disapproval and, on their advice, he abandoned his daydream though he still made an effort to visit it, despite the fact that it was now damaged and empty and the glass in its windows was broken.

It was the same kind of frustration and melancholy that he associated with his night dreams of Asolo, the little hill town he had first seen (and then only at a distance), when he was twenty-six years old. Since that time, and for no rational reason, it had appeared over and over in the poet's dreams as a destination on the horizon, one that, due to a variety of circumstances, he was never able to reach. Either his companions in the dream would persuade him to take an alternate route, or the road would be impassable, or he would awaken just as the town gate came into view, frustrated and out of sorts. 'I've had my old Asolo dream again,' he would tell his sister at breakfast, 'and it has no doubt ruined my work for the whole day.'

Then, just last summer, he had spent several months there at the home of a friend. The house was charming and the view of the valley delighted him. But, although he never once broke the well-established order that ruled the days of his life, a sense of unreality clouded his perceptions. He was visiting the memory of a dream with a major and important difference. He had reached the previously elusive hill town with practically no effort. Everything had proceeded according to plan. Thinking about this, under the December sky in Venice, Browning realized that he had known since then that it was only going to be a matter of time.

The gondola bumped against the steps of his son's palazzo.

Robert Browning climbed onto the terrace, paid the gondolier, and walked briskly inside.

LYING ON THE magnificent carved bed in his room, trying unsuccessfully to surrender himself to his regular pre-dinner nap, Robert Browning examined his knowledge like a stolen jewel he had coveted for years; turning it first this way, then that, imagining the reactions of his friends, what his future biographers would have to say about it all. He was pleased that he had prudently written his death poem at Asolo in direct response to having received a copy of Tennyson's 'Crossing the

Bar' in the mail. How he detested that poem! What *could* Alfred have been thinking of when he wrote it? He had to admit, none the less, that to suggest that mourners restrain their sorrow, as Tennyson had, guarantees the floodgates of female tears will eventually burst open. His poem had, therefore, included similar sentiments, but without, he hoped, such obvious sentimentality. It was the final poem of his last manuscript which was now, mercifully, at the printers.

Something for the biographers and for the weeping maidens; those who had wept so copiously for his dear departed, though soon to be reinstated wife. Surely it was not too much to ask that they might shed a few tears for him as well, even if it was a more ordinary death, following, he winced to have to add, a fairly conventional life.

How had it all happened? He had placed himself in the centre of some of the world's most exotic scenery and had then lived his life there with the regularity of a copy clerk. A time for everything, everything in its time. Even when hunting for lizards in Asolo, an occupation he considered slightly exotic, he found he could predict the moment of their appearance; as if they knew he was searching for them and assembled their modest population at the sound of his footsteps. Even so, he was able to flush out only six or seven from a hedge of considerable length and these were, more often than not, of the same type. Once he thought he had seen a particularly strange lizard, large and lumpy, but it had turned out to be merely two of the ordinary sort, copulating.

Copulation. What sad dirge-like associations the word dredged up from the poet's unconscious. All those Italians; those minstrels, dukes, princes, artists, and questionable monks whose voices had droned through Browning's pen over the years. Why had they all been so endlessly obsessed with the subject? He could never understand or control it. And even now, one of them had appeared in full period costume in his imagination. A duke, no doubt, by the look of the yards of velvet which covered his person. He was reading a letter that was causing him a great deal of pain. Was it a letter from his mistress? A draught of poison waited on an intricately tooled small table to his left. Perhaps a pistol or a dagger as well, but in this light Browning could not quite tell. The man paced, paused, looked wistfully out the window as if waiting for someone he knew would never, ever appear. Very, very soon now he would begin to speak, to tell his story. His right hand passed nervously across his eyes. He turned to look directly at Robert Browning who, as always, was beginning to feel somewhat embarrassed. Then the duke began:

> *At last to leave these darkening moments*
> *These rooms, these halls where once*
> *We stirred love's poisoned potions*
> *The deepest of all slumbers,*
> *After this astounds the mummers*
> *I cannot express the smile that circled*
> *Round and round the week*
> *This room and all our days when morning*
> *Entered, soft, across her cheek.*
> *She was my medallion, my caged dove,*
> *A trinket, a coin I carried warm,*
> *Against the skin inside my glove*
> *My favourite artwork was a kind of jail*
> *Our portrait permanent, imprinted by the moon*
> *Upon the ancient face of the canal.*

The man began to fade. Browning, who had not invited him into the room in the first place, was already bored. He therefore dismissed the crimson costume, the table, the potion housed in its delicate goblet of fine Venetian glass and began, quite inexplicably, to think about Percy Bysshe Shelley; about his life, and under the circumstances, more importantly, about his death.

DINNER OVER, sister, son and daughter-in-law and friend all chatted with and later read to, Browning returned to his room with Shelley's death hovering around him like an annoying, directionless wind. He doubted, as he put on his nightgown, that Shelley had *ever* worn one, particularly in those dramatic days preceding his early demise. In his night-cap he felt as ridiculous as a humorous political drawing for *Punch* magazine. And, as he lumbered into bed alone, he remembered that Shelley would have had Mary beside him and possibly Clare as well, their minds buzzing with nameless Gothic terrors. For a desperate moment or two Browning tried to conjure a Gothic terror but discovered, to his great disappointment, that the vague shape taking form in his mind was only his dreary Italian duke coming, predictably, once again into focus.

Outside the ever calm waters of the canal licked the edge of the terrace in a rhythmic, sleep-inducing manner; a restful sound guaranteeing peace of mind. Browning knew, however, that during Shelley's last days at Lerici, giant waves had crashed into the ground floor of Casa Magni, prefiguring the young poet's violent death and causing his sleep to be riddled with wonderful nightmares. Therefore, the very lack of activity on the part of the water below irritated the old man. He began to pad around the room in his bare feet, oblivious of the cold marble floor and the dying embers in the fireplace. He peered through the windows into the night, hoping that he, like Shelley, might at least see his double there, or possibly Elizabeth's ghost beckoning to him from the centre of the canal. He cursed softly as the night gazed back at him, serene and cold and entirely lacking in events – mysterious or otherwise.

He returned to the bed and knelt by its edge in order to say his evening prayers. But he was completely unable to concentrate. Shelley's last days were trapped in his brain like fish in a tank. He saw him surrounded by the sublime scenery of the Ligurian coast, searching the horizon for the boat that was to be his coffin. Then he saw him clinging desperately to the mast of that boat while lightning tore the sky in half and the ocean spilled across the hull. Finally, he saw Shelley's horrifying corpse rolling on the shoreline, practically unidentifiable except for the copy of Keats' poems housed in his breast pocket. *Next to his heart,* Byron had commented, just before he got to work on the funeral pyre.

Browning abandoned God for the moment and climbed beneath the blankets.

'I might at least have a nightmare,' he said petulantly to himself. Then he fell into a deep and dreamless sleep.

BROWNING AWAKENED the next morning with an itchy feeling
in his throat and lines from Shelley's *Prometheus Unbound*
dancing in his head.

'Oh, God,' he groaned inwardly, 'now this. And I don't even
like Shelley's poetry any more. Now I suppose I'm going to be
plagued with it, day in, day out, until the instant of my immi-
nent death.'

How he wished he had never, ever, been fond of Shelley's
poems. Then, in his youth, he might have had the common
sense *not* to read them compulsively to the point of total recall.
But how could he have known in those early days that even
though he would later come to reject both Shelley's life and
work as being too impossibly self-absorbed and emotional,
some far corner of his brain would still retain every syllable the
young man had committed to paper. He had memorized his
life's work. Shortly after Browning's memory recited *The
crawling glaciers pierce me with spears / Of their moon freezing crys-
tals, the bright chains / Eat with their burning cold into my bones,*
he began to cough, a spasm that lasted until his sister knocked
discreetly on the door to announce that, since he had not
appeared downstairs, his breakfast was waiting on a tray in the
hall.

While he was drinking his tea, the poem 'Ozymandias'
repeated itself four times in his mind except that, to his great
annoyance, he found that he could not remember the last three
lines and kept ending with *Look on my works, ye Mighty, and
despair.* He knew for certain that there were three more lines,
but he was damned if he could recall even one of them. He
thought of asking his sister but soon realized that, since she
was familiar with his views on Shelley, he would be forced to
answer a series of embarrassing questions about why he was
thinking about the poem at all. Finally, he decided that *Look on
my works, ye Mighty, and despair* was a much more fitting ending to the poem and attributed his lack of recall to the supposi-
tion that the last three lines were either unsuitable or completely unimportant. That settled, he wolfed down his roll,
donned his hat and coat, and departed for the streets in hopes
that something, anything, might happen.

Even years later, Browning's sister and son could still be

counted upon to spend a full evening discussing what he might have done that day. The possibilities were endless. He might have gone off hunting for a suitable setting for a new poem, or for the physical characteristics of a duke by examining handsome northern Italian workmen. He might have gone, again, to visit his beloved Palazzo Manzoni, to gaze wistfully at its marble medallions. He might have gone to visit a Venetian builder, to discuss plans for the beautiful tower he had talked about building at Asolo, or out to Murano to watch men mould their delicate bubbles of glass. His sister was convinced that he had gone to the Church of S.S. Giovanni e Paolo to gaze at his favourite equestrian statue. His pious son, on the other hand, liked to believe that his father had spent the day in one of the few English churches in Venice, praying for the redemption of his soul. But all of their speculations assumed a sense of purpose on the poet's part, that he had left the house with a definite destination in mind, because as long as they could remember, he had never acted without a predetermined plan.

Without a plan, Robert Browning faced the Grand Canal with very little knowledge of what, in fact, he was going to do. He looked to the left, and then to the right, and then, waving aside an expectant gondolier, he turned abruptly and entered the thick of the city behind him. There he wandered aimlessly through a labyrinth of narrow streets, noting details; *putti* wafting stone garlands over windows, door knockers in the shape of gargoyles' heads, painted windows that fooled the eye, items that two weeks earlier would have delighted him but now seemed used and lifeless. Statues appeared to leak and ooze damp soot, window-glass was fogged with moisture, steps that led him over canals were slippery, covered with an unhealthy slime. He became peculiarly aware of smells he had previously ignored in favour of the more pleasant sensations the city had to offer. But now even the small roof gardens seemed to grow as if in stagnant water, winter chrysanthemums emitting a putrid odour, which spoke less of blossom than decay. With a kind of slow horror, Browning realized that he was seeing his beloved city through Shelley's eyes and immediately his inner voice began again: *Sepulchres where human forms / Like pollution nourished worms / To the corpse of greatness cling / Murdered and now mouldering.*

He quickened his steps, hoping that if he concentrated on physical activity his mind would not subject him to the complete version of Shelley's 'Lines Written Among the Euganean Hills.' But he was not to be spared. The poem had been one of his favourites in his youth and, as a result, his mind was now capable of reciting it to him, word by word, with appropriate emotional inflections, followed by a particularly moving rendition of 'Julian and Maddalo' accompanied by mental pictures of Shelley and Byron galloping along the beach at the Lido.

When at last the recitation ceased, Browning had walked as far as possible and now found himself at the edge of the Fondamente Nuove with only the wide flat expanse of the Laguna Morta in front of him.

He surveyed his surroundings and began, almost unconsciously, and certainly against his will, to search for the islanded madhouse that Shelley had described in 'Julian and Maddalo': *A building on an island; such a one / As age to age might add, for uses vile / A windowless, deformed and dreary pile.* Then he remembered, again against his will, that it was on the other side, near the Lido. Instead, his eyes came to rest on the cemetery island of San Michele whose neat white mausoleums and tidy cypresses looked fresher, less sepulchral than any portion of the city he had passed through. Although he had never been there, he could tell, even from this distance, that its paths would be raked and its marble scrubbed in a way that the rest of Venice never was. Like a disease that cannot cross the water, the rot and mould of the city had never reached the cemetery's shore.

It pleased Browning, now, to think of the island's clean-boned inhabitants sleeping in their white-washed houses. Then, his mood abruptly changing, he thought with disgust of Shelley, of his bloated corpse upon the sands, how his flesh had been saturated by water, then burned away by fire, and how his heart had refused to burn, as if it had not been made of flesh at all.

Browning felt the congestion in his chest take hold, making his breathing shallow and laboured, and he turned back into the city, attempting to determine the direction of his son's palazzo. Pausing now and then to catch his breath, he made his way slowly through the streets that make up the Fondamente Nuove, an area with which he was completely unfamiliar. This was Venice at its most squalid. What little elegance had originally existed in this section had now faded so dramatically that it had all but disappeared. Scrawny children screamed and giggled on every narrow walkway and tattered washing hung from most windows. In doorways, sullen elderly widows stared insolently and with increasing hostility at this obvious foreigner who had invaded their territory. A dull panic began to overcome him as he realized he was lost. The disease meanwhile had weakened his legs, and he stumbled awkwardly under the communal gaze of these women who were like black angels marking his path. Eager to be rid of their judgemental stares, he turned into an alley, smaller than the last, and found to his relief that it was deserted and graced with a small fountain and a stone bench.

The alley, of course, was blind, went nowhere, but it was peaceful and Browning was in need of rest. He leaned back against the stone wall and closed his eyes. The fountain murmured *Bysshe, Bysshe, Bysshe* until the sound finally became soothing to Browning and he dozed, on and off, while fragments of Shelley's poetry moved in and out of his consciousness.

Then, waking suddenly from one of these moments of semi-slumber, he began to feel again that he was being watched. He searched the upper windows and the doorways around him for old women and found none. Instinctively, he looked at an archway which was just a fraction to the left of his line of vision. There, staring directly into his own, was the face of Percy Bysshe Shelley, as young and sad and powerful as Browning had ever known it would be. The visage gained flesh and expression for a glorious thirty seconds before returning to the marble that it really was. With a sickening and familiar sense of loss, Browning recognized the carving of Dionysus, or Pan, or Adonis, that often graced the tops of Venetian doorways. The sick old man walked toward it and, reaching up, placed his fingers on the soiled cheek. 'Suntreader,' he mumbled, then he moved out of the alley, past the black, disapproving women, into the streets towards a sizeable canal. There, bent over his walking stick, coughing spasmodically, he was able to hail a gondola.

All the way back across the city he murmured, 'Where have you been, where have you been, where did you go?'

ROBERT BROWNING lay dying in his son's Venetian palazzo. Half of his face was shaded by a large velvet curtain which was gathered by his shoulder, the other half lay exposed to the weak winter light. His sister, son, and daughter-in-law stood at the foot of the bed nervously awaiting words or signs from the old man. They spoke to each other silently by means of glances or gestures, hoping they would not miss any kind of signal from his body, mountain-like under the white bedclothes. But for hours now nothing had happened. Browning's large chest moved up and down in a slow and rhythmic fashion, not unlike an artificially manipulated bellows. He appeared to be unconscious.

But Browning was not unconscious. Rather, he had used the last remnants of his free will to make a final decision. There were to be no last words. How inadequate his words seemed now compared to Shelley's experience, how silly this monotonous bedridden death. He did not intend to further add to the absurdity by pontificating. He now knew that he had said too much. At this very moment, in London, a volume of superfluous words was coming off the press. All this chatter filling up the space of Shelley's more important silence. He now knew that when Shelley had spoken it was by choice and not by habit, that the young man's words had been a response and not a fabrication.

He opened his eyes a crack and found himself staring at the ceiling. The fresco there moved and changed and finally evolved into Shelley's iconography – an eagle struggling with a serpent. *Suntreader*. The clouds, the white foam of the clouds, like water, the feathers of the great wings becoming lost in this. *Half angel, half bird*. And the blue of the sky, opening now, erasing the ceiling, limitless so that the bird's wing seemed to vaporize. *A moulted feather, an eagle feather*. Such untravelled distance in which light arrived and disappeared leaving behind something that was not darkness. *His radiant form becoming less radiant.* Leaving its own natural absence with the strength and the suck of a vacuum. No alternate atmosphere to fill the place abandoned. *Suntreader.*

And now Browning understood. It was Shelley's absence he had carried with him all these years until it had passed beyond his understanding. *Soft star.* Shelley's emotions so absent from the old poet's life, his work, leaving him unanswered, speaking through the mouths of others, until he had to turn away from Shelley altogether in anger and disgust. The drowned spirit had outdistanced him wherever he sought it. *Lone and sunny idleness of heaven.* The anger, the disgust, the evaporation. *Suntreader, soft star.* The formless form he never possessed and was never possessed by.

Too weak for anger now, Robert Browning closed his eyes and relaxed his fists, allowing Shelley's corpse to enter the place in his imagination where once there had been only absence. It floated through the sea of Browning's mind, its muscles soft under the constant pressure of the ocean. Limp and drifting, the drowned man looked as supple as a mermaid, arms swaying in the current, hair and clothing tossed as if in a slow, slow wind. His body was losing colour, turning from pastel to opaque, the open eyes staring, pale, as if frozen by an image of the moon. Joints unlocked by moisture, limbs swung easy on their threads of tendon, the spine undulating and relaxed. The absolute grace of this death, that life caught there moving in the arms of the sea. Responding, always responding to the elements.

Now the drowned poet began to move into a kind of Atlantis consisting of Browning's dream architecture; the unobtainable and the unconstructed. In complete silence the young man swam through the rooms of the Palazzo Manzoni, slipping up and down the staircase, gliding down halls, in and out of fireplaces. He appeared briefly in mirrors. He drifted past balconies to the tower Browning had thought of building at Asolo. He wavered for a few minutes near its crenellated peak before moving in a slow spiral down along its edges to its base.

Browning had just enough time to wish for the drama and the luxury of a death by water. Then his fading attention was caught by the rhythmic bump of a moored gondola against the terrace below. The boat was waiting, he knew, to take his body to the cemetery at San Michele when the afternoon had passed. Shelley had said somewhere that a gondola was a butterfly of which the coffin was a chrysalis.

Suntreader. Still beyond his grasp. The eagle on the ceiling lost in unfocused fog. *A moulted feather, an eagle feather, well I forget the rest.* The drowned man's body separated into parts and moved slowly out of Browning's mind. The old poet contented himself with the thought of one last journey by water. The coffin boat, the chrysalis. Across the Laguna Morta to San Michele. All that cool white marble in exchange for the shifting sands of Lerici.

Forbidden Dances

MY GRANDMOTHER never went to dances; not as a young girl and certainly not later. Her father, whom I imagined as a beak-nosed, square-jawed individual with a Bible in one hand and a whip in the other, absolutely forbade it because of the Devil who was well known to enter even the most Methodist of households once the dancing began. I remember her telling me this in her linoleum-and-wallpapered kitchen, and I remember that when she told it, not a hint of amusement entered her voice. Instead, there was the rumour of sadness and resignation that accompanies the confession of a joy wished for, anticipated, but never experienced and then out of reach forever.

'He absolutely forbade it,' she would say, twitching a little in her rocker, nervous as a young girl who is waiting to be asked to dance and who knows she never will be.

I had never heard the word *forbid* spoken aloud before, though of course, I had read it in novels. My own parents used words like *won't* and *can't* and *it's not allowed. I'm not allowed to,* I had always told friends who wanted me to cross busy roads, or walk over railway trestles, or travel by subway into the dark heart of the city. It was a sentence connected to time. I knew the word *not* would disappear in a few years and the possibilities of the word *allow* would open up. *Forbid* was a closed, sealed and bolted door.

Grandma lived in the village where she was born, in the large frame house that my grandfather had purchased after he had retired and my uncle had taken over the family farm. You could see the outer fields of the farm from Grandma's kitchen windows and sometimes my uncle as well going back and forth across them on his red tractor. Grandma was able, therefore, to supervise some farming activities through glass, the way signalmen in their wooden towers supervise trains. This occasionally caused her anxiety. 'I hope,' she would say, looking out the south window and letting the piece of cotton she was working on slip onto her lap, 'I hope Arnold gets the hay in before it rains, before it's too late.'

Every facet of the landscape that surrounded her house was steeped in memory for Grandma. All she had to do, to move from married life to childhood, was walk from the south side of the kitchen to the north and settle herself in a different chair. From her north window she could see the monumental hill that loomed up behind the house and barn her forbidding father had owned. Once, when she was a young girl, she had been sent to fetch six or seven cows from the top of that hill and one of them had stumbled and fallen, a blur of black and white, all the way down to its death. Was it her fault? I wondered. Was that why her father forbade her to dance?

She preferred the south side of the kitchen despite the fact that the view from there was a constant reminder of the ever present possibility of crop failure. She preferred it, I assumed, to the memory of a hard climb, a tragic fall, and forbidden dances. Only recently did it occur to me that she probably sat there because the light was better and, since her eyesight was failing, it was becoming more and more difficult for her to work on whatever piece of appliquéd patchwork she was sewing at the time. She had never been much good at needlework, which was odd because she was always at it. This was an activity, she told me, that her father approved of, insisted upon, actually. An enforced pastime that must, despite her lack of skill, have developed into a habit. Her house was crammed with rather shoddy examples of this work; appliquéd quilts on the beds, sloppy cross-stitching on the pillows, embroidered runners on the sideboards. And all the same motif – fabric ladies in long pastel dresses who looked as if they might be preparing to go to a dance, even though the stitches that held them together were unlikely to endure long enough to get them there.

Grandma often sighed as she moved her fingers through her work basket looking for a certain shade of embroidery thread or the right piece of calico. She sighed and looked out the window and worried about the crops. When she began to sew she moved one black-laced shoe up and down in a rhythmic manner as if she were keeping time to some mysterious inner music. Then with her back to that ominous, dangerous hill, she told me stories of her girlhood.

It wasn't until I was almost fully grown, however, that she told me what had happened to her best friend – the girl who *had* gone to the dances.

GRANDMA'S KITCHEN was filled with knick-knacks, bric-à-brac, little tributes to domesticity, little prayers painted on glass. *Oh, Lord of pots and pans and things / Give me comfort, give me wings.* And there were instructions and recipes for wifedom as well, burned into thin wooden plaques. *Thirty pounds of industry, thirty pounds of prudence, fifteen pounds of good humour, fifteen pounds of necessary pride.*

'What is prudence, Grandma?'

'Prudence,' said Grandma, 'is what my best friend had very little of. Oh, she was beautiful all right, and she could dance, but she was not prudent. Did I ever tell you about the runaway horses?'

'No,' I said, lying, because I wanted to hear the story again.

'We were twelve and her father had let us take the horses and the cutter to Centerton, at night, mind you. My father would never let me take horses anywhere, any time. Women's hands are not made for reins and whips, he said to me.' Grandma walked across the room and opened the curtains that covered the north window as if the view out there were a stage on which this particular drama was to be acted out. Then she began to clear the breakfast dishes from the table.

'So we went there, visited someone ... I don't remember who ... and on the way back the horses ran away with us.'

'Did she make them run away, Grandma?'

'No, but she let them run away which is just as bad or maybe worse. So there we were, two young girls, streaking across the snowy fields in the dark. She thought they'd stop at the fence but what she didn't know and what I *did* know is that a runaway horse doesn't even see a fence.'

'What happened?'

'Nothing much because of the snow. The fence was damaged, the cutter was damaged but we, and the horses, were fine. She just sat there laughing to beat the band, up to her waist in snow.'

I smiled, imagining Grandma's best friend in her dancing attire laughing in a moonlit drift.

'But you couldn't call that prudent, now, could you,' said Grandma, 'being so carefree and all about runaway horses and fences? No,' she answered herself thoughtfully, 'you couldn't call that prudent at all.'

ACROSS THE ROAD from Grandma's house, behind an abandoned turnip factory, was a woods filled with a series of wonders entirely formed by water. The *crick,* as Grandma called it, wound through this shady territory expanding at times to form deep black pools and then contracting again to dance in a reckless fashion over pastel-coloured pebbles. Spending a lot of time in this spot, which was sealed off by cedars from the rest of the world, was not forbidden by Grandma and so all through my childhood visits I made daily treks down there to watch water spiders tango across the little ponds and to observe the plentiful trout perform their sinuous gavotte. Dragonflies waltzed over water, their wings like taffeta skirts. Down there, in there, everything appeared to be dancing. Everything but my own reflection on the surface of a small dark pool. Both my reflection and I were merely watching; watching and waiting for something, anything, to ask us to dance.

Returning from that cool place I could see Grandma's square frame house, sturdy as a fortress, across the road. The straight lines of its clapboard, the clean gleam of its windows. I can see it now, too. Even after all these years it is a memory so vivid I can walk through its rooms any time I choose and examine its contents the way I did when I was a child. This was an activity of which I never tired and another that was not forbidden. I learned about my deceased grandfather through his untidy desk whose drawers contained I.O.U.s and farmer's almanacs and worthless insurance policies and dried-out rubber bands and Victory Bonds and Liberal Party newsletters, and through the stern bearded gentlemen who adorned his unused Gillette razor blades. My two mysterious dead uncles I came to know by investigating their mutual bedroom which revealed a closet full of World-War-Two uniforms and dresser drawers rife with the strange things young men keep; match-books, theatre stubs, marbles, coins, sticks of old rigid chewing gum, single cuff links, garish bow ties. And by just staying in that house, by sleeping under its quilts and resting my head on its embroidered pillows, I became acquainted with Grandma's best friend. Because, you see, she *was* that endless series of pastel-clothed girls that my grandmother so awkwardly, and so obstinately, created.

MY OWN FIRST DANCE is a memory that I'd rather turn away from; turn away from the dark pool of dancing, walk back along the cedar-lined path towards the kitchen, the sunlight, the linoleum. I really *liked* that linoleum. I liked the battered tins filled with oatmeal cookies too, and the old wood stove in whose warming oven I could dry my shoes if I had slipped into the crick while attempting to cross it on a log. I liked all of Grandma's house right down to the last pearl button, forgot-ten and wedged between the slats of a bedroom drawer. I liked the old Christmas cards and the strange striped suspenders that hung, untouched for years, on hooks at the far end of clothes cupboards. I even liked the cluster flies that remained, brittle and dead, on the sills of windows in the vacant bedrooms. I liked all of this but I did not like my first dance.

I was not asked of course, and wouldn't have known how to dance even if I had been. Yet it was a deep, deep pool, that basement of what was, ironically, a Methodist church, where everything moved but me.

The still pool of my shame growing darker and darker as the evening progressed until I wasn't sure whether I had become it or was merely reflected upon its surface. The girls I knew float-ing around the room in pastel dresses, just grazing the surface like dragonflies; their thin, young partners as awkward and as beautiful as water spiders – God, how I wished my father had forbidden the whole thing.

SHE WAS VERY BEAUTIFUL, this friend my Grandma draughted

on swaths of fabric, over and over, in her spare time, distracted only now and then by a threat of hail or a fear of drought. She was very beautiful, said Grandma, owned beautiful pastel dresses and could dance like the wind though Grandma had never seen this because it was forbidden. Poor Grandma was more concerned at that stage of her life with the exact black and white of a dead cow than the way dusty rose or powder blue looks when you move inside it across an oak wood floor. More concerned, I suppose, with getting those cumbersome beasts down that terrifying hill without killing them.

Grandma's friend had danced and danced in her soft yellow dresses, her dusty rose, her taffeta ...

The dark pool that was at the heart of me was not asked to dance for a long, long time. You remember, the one surrounded by cedars, the one where the sun is shut out, the one you leave the bright blaze of the kitchen for. That one was not asked to dance, no, not for a long, long time. The request was finally made, however, and not by anything that hovered or scuttled over the surface either. This had nothing to do with taffeta, or even oak wood floors. The request was made slowly, gracefully, and deeply.

Come down. Come down.

'SHE WAS VERY BEAUTIFUL,' said Grandma, 'she went to dances and she drowned.'

I was fifteen, had stopped exploring the house, but had not stopped visiting the chain of pools.

'How did she drown, Grandma?'

'She drowned,' said Grandma, picking a bright yellow strand of embroidery thread from her basket and holding it with the needle to the light. 'She drowned herself.'

Drowning ... dancing.

'There was a man,' said Grandma. 'A man she wasn't married to. He left town.'

'Did she never marry, then?'

'No.' Grandma cut out a miniature yellow skirt with her sharp scissors. 'No ... she was already married.'

'But you said she wasn't married to him.'

'That's right,' said Grandma, placing the skirt on a soft mauve ground, 'She was married to somebody else.'

'Was it the dancing?' I asked urgently, the memory of my own first dance still sharp and painful in my mind.

'I suppose that must have been part of it,' sighed Grandma.

It was late afternoon. The kitchen was turning shades of blue and grey. Grandma stopped her handiwork for a moment, two or three completed dancers on her lap, and looked out the window towards the fields. There was a threat of storm on the horizon. I could hear the hum of my uncle's tractor.

'Grandma,' I asked, 'Grandma, why did he leave town?'

'He left town,' she replied, putting away the fabric, the scissors, the thread, 'because he was finished with her.'

I immediately thought of the room upstairs that had been inhabited by my two dead uncles while they were still alive. I thought about the foreignness of it, the strangeness – how they kept things that wouldn't have interested me in the least, those matchbooks and baseball cards. And the male smell of them still there after years of absence: sweat in a glove, stains under the arms of their uniforms. How odd it was, how other. How unlike Grandma's room with Grandpa gone. A room that smelled of lavender and wild rose sachets. A room ... a room ...

Yes, I thought, he would keep the oddest things and he would throw away Grandma's best friend ... the dusty rose ... the lavender.

LET'S LOOK OUT the north window towards Grandma's girlhood. How tidy its fields are, how docile its well-behaved, fenced horses. In front of the barn are six clean, perfect cows and behind it that hill, blocking the view to anywhere else.

When I looked out that window I imagined him as a large and fearsome trout of odd foreign colours attracted by a bright fly, then, perceiving the hook attached, vanishing into a far corner of the pond where he could never be found.

When I looked out the south window I imagined him to be shiftless, uncaring – a shirker of duty, a handsome heartbreaker. More like a fickle, skittish water spider, darting from place to place, never fixed or settled.

It seems I spent a great deal of my girlhood imagining him as one thing or another. But either way I always imagined him gone.

I knew all about Ophelia, of course, all about the Lady of Shalott. All through my girlhood I had sympathized with their long, sad journeys on rivers; journeys taken after they had been discarded. In my mind's eye they always looked to me like beautiful refuse in the water, bright bits of garbage, everything trailing and coming apart at the seams. Hair, shawls, arms, fingers. I loved the way they never even tried to swim ... just let the river carry them along on their last, broken solitary voyage. Yes, I knew all about them. Still, after Grandma told me, it wasn't them I was looking for while I walked through knee-high ferns, down the cedar-lined path towards the dark transparent water. It wasn't them. It was Grandma's best friend.

'FOR A FEW MONTHS afterwards,' continued Grandma, empty-handed now, rocking in her chair, 'several of the women in town would rise and leave the church if ever she came in, but only a few months afterwards because there only *were* a few months afterwards.' The black shoe at the end of her lisle stocking moved quickly up and down. The music that I couldn't hear had increased in tempo.

'Why did they do that, Grandma?' I was visualizing a dark congregation and Grandma's best friend, the only pastel flower, waltzing down the aisle.

'They did that,' said Grandma, 'because they *knew* and they felt they had to register their disapproval.'

'Did her husband leave with them?'

'No, her husband stayed with her. But he knew, too, there was no doubt of that. He just stayed with her all the time. They were always together.'

'At the dances?'

'There were no more dances, at least for them. There were never any for me. My father forbade it.' Grandma walked across the room to the north window and stared, for just a moment, almost angrily, at her girlhood.

'He absolutely forbade it,' she said.

GRANDMA HAD BEEN DEAD for some time before the dark pool at the heart of me was asked to dance. I had been responsible for selling her house. Farewell to the linoleum and cookie tins, farewell to her lavender and cluster flies, the Gillette razor blades, still there, still wrapped. Farewell to the north window of her girlhood and the south window of her married life, her rocking chair, her warming oven, her cupboards. Farewell to her bright, warm kitchen. But not farewell to her best friend. I took some of her with me; a quilt, an embroidered runner, a cutting of pastel cotton.

I took those items and a memory of a chain of dark pools. I hadn't asked Grandma where her best friend drowned because I'd seen her down there many times, gazing back at me as I stared into the water – a water spider dancing on her forehead, a trout passing obsessively back and forth behind her eyes. Until I reached for him once and he moved into that distant corner where he could never be found.

I took some other objects, as well, from Grandma's kitchen and placed them in my own when I finally got one. They looked uncomfortable there, difficult – the wooden plaques, the salt and pepper shakers. Eventually it seemed imperative that I remove them. But by then I wasn't spending a lot of time in the kitchen. By then that dark part of me had accepted an invitation. I'd started dancing.

AUTUMN AND EARLY EVENING at Grandma's house. She was working on the surface of a cotton apron where six pastel ladies danced on a pure white ground. Outside, the north hill of her girlhood glowed as if all light and attention were focused on it and the south fields of her married life lay covered by the long shadows of the surrounding trees. I was reading a Victorian girl's book that had flowers on its embossed cover and words like *forbid* on its cream-coloured pages.

Grandma rose from her rocking chair and walked across the room to the upright cupboard in the corner. From one of its two drawers she removed an ivory-coloured box and, after lifting the lid, she placed it on my lap so that I could look at the contents as though I had never seen them before.

Brittle, broken, faded, I thought.

'That,' said Grandma, 'is my wedding bouquet.'

'I know,' I said.

I knew about her wedding gown too which was upstairs in the storeroom and which I had tried on every year since I was five years old. It lay, folded, in an old brown trunk together with some pillow shams that Grandma had begun to sew before her wedding, which (perhaps because their embroidered design contained no pastel ladies) she had never finished.

'My wedding gown is upstairs in the storeroom,' said Grandma. She paused and examined her hands, first from the front, then from the back. 'I was very happy,' she said.

The book I was reading concerned a young girl who had forsaken her true love in order to nurse her aged parents. 'Alas, I cannot marry,' she had just said. *Forsake* was another one of those words that hardly anyone had ever spoken aloud in my presence.

I handed the boxed bouquet back to Grandma. She stood in her green kitchen and stared down at its faded colours. Then she returned it to the drawer.

'And one more thing ...,' she said.

I looked up from my book.

'I was one of the women ... one of the women who walked out of the church.'

YEARS GO BY and the furnishings of the past are scattered. Landscapes are altered. A kitchen fades into the night and smooth highways invade leafy places. Hastily made quilts disintegrate in the washing machine and all the dancing ladies come apart at the seams.

A request is finally made, however, and when it is you recognize it immediately. Runaway horses crash through unseen fences, dance floors appear where they have absolutely no right to be, chains of dark pools unfurl across the forehead. Then a dancer beckons from moist hidden places and the world is shut out.

When he leaves me, Grandma, which will be very, very soon now, I know exactly what I'll do. Goodbye to the north light of girlhood, the south light of married life. Farewell to the relics in vacant bedrooms: the lavender and talc. I'll put on that pastel dress you made for me, Grandma, with its loose stitches and ill-fitting sleeves, its crooked hem and sloppy embroidery. I'll leave behind your kitchen and walk beside the dancing crick, along the cedar-lined path, down to the dark heart of the pool I have become.

She'll be waiting for me there, Grandma, she always was. Together we'll recall forbidden dances.

Seven Confessions

Merry-Go-Round with Approaching Storm

GLUTTONY

I WAS ALREADY HUNGRY by the time we entered our room at about four in the afternoon. Even though we had had seven different kinds of cheese, a loaf of very good bread, some regional pâté, and a full bottle of red Burgundy at our picnic lunch, I was definitely hungry. Besides, I could smell activity in the kitchen below, could even hear utensils being moved around. All that stainless steel.

The room was familiar, one-star, French. Charm verging on kitsch, floating roses on the wallpaper, the inevitable bidet, and a bed, supposed to be a double, but with an indentation in the middle, where I imagined hundreds of lonely single men had slept, leaving their permanent mark.

'Why not women?' he asked when I pointed this out to him.

'Women don't go to hotels when they're lonely,' I said, 'at least not alone.'

Outside, the town was very busy. Diesel fumes hung in the air. Trucks delivered merchandise, waiters rushed from table to table at the café across the street, swarms of motorcycles buzzed like angry bees.

'They sound like bees,' I said.

'Who?' he replied.

I looked at the lace curtains. They were as precise as snowflakes on either side of the glass and as indistinguishable from each other, except at close range. I knew that when we went for a walk (we always went for a walk), I would be unable to pick out our window from the opposite side of the street. That's the way it always was. I would try and be wrong, because the curtains always looked the same.

He called the desk and asked about dinner. 'Eight o'clock,' he said as he hung up the phone. At that moment, the table in the hotel restaurant presented itself to my imagination; those plates in front of me, two, sometimes three on top of each other, sometimes with flowers painted on them, sometimes with peacocks. And heavy tableware, almost too large for my mouth, so that soup could be finished in three spoonfuls. I tried not to spill. But he didn't care, left evidence of each course on the tablecloth. Nothing much, but still I noticed and wondered about hotel laundries.

I opened the door of the large wooden wardrobe, looking for real pillows. We could never sleep with our heads propped on those funny loglike bolsters that the French somehow managed to wrap the bottom sheet around. As I reached up to the top shelf where two square feather pillows were waiting, empty hangers jangled on a wooden pole. This hotel doesn't care about their hangers, I thought. I had been in other, less trusting establishments where the hangers were made out of stainless steel and could not be removed without a hacksaw. Until then I had never considered stealing a hanger, but when I saw them dangling there, irremovable, I could suddenly imagine myself slinking across a parking lot at two o'clock in the morning, delicate metal objects jingling like wind chimes in my hand. Sirens in the distance.

'Shall we go for a walk?' he suggested.

Going somewhere from one of those hotels always meant down. Returning always meant up. So we went down the hall, down the stairs, and down the street. Down, down, into the centre of town. Here, as in most other French towns of any size whatsoever, was a narrow, park-like area situated in the centre of the main boulevard. It was edged by a series of strange trees, pollarded into grotesque shapes. In front of these, facing the traffic, green benches were placed at regular intervals. The ground was covered with a thin layer of gravel from which a workman, dressed in blue, was industriously raking footprints and the outlines of a child's game. The low sun threw the shadows of iron wastebaskets to such a length that they touched as if reaching hands toward each other.

Walking through the middle of this towards the end of town, he decided that he liked the trees.

'I like these trees,' he said, 'because they do not look to me at all like trees. They look like the skeletons of umbrellas in the dump. They look like they have had arthritis for a long, long time. They look like spiders with tumors on their elbows.' (By this time he was setting up his tripod.) 'They look like what the bone structure of octopi would look like if octopi had bones. I am very, very fond of these trees.'

'I think,' I replied, 'that they should leave it all alone.' I meant the trees, the footprints, the child's game, the wastebaskets' shadows.

'Who are *they*?' he asked.

This kind of question was designed by him to put a stop to any monologue that might have been cooking in my head. He could sense these monologues in advance, knew when they were about to come creeping into a walk, or a meal, or even a drive in the car. The trouble with the monologues, he had told me, was that although they started quietly, they quickly escalated, turning from apparent reverie to obvious accusation. This bored him. He hated my monologues. Put a stop to them, was his motto, before they go too far. Nip them in the bud with unanswerable questions. This time the echoes asked, *Why do they do it? Why do they do it?* They became fainter and fainter, however, and finally disappeared altogether.

While he photographed the trees, I sat down on one of the green benches and searched through my cluttered purse for a pen and a piece of scrap paper. I was going to sketch the stone wall on the other side of the street. I had never done this before. I had never sketched anything. But now I wanted to. Not that the wall was worth sketching; it was just that there was absolutely nothing linear about its surface, making it impossible for anyone without skill to render it at all. Now I wanted to try something impossible, something I could work on for a while and then throw away saying, *this is impossible.* Something where the outcome was certain.

He had attached a telephoto lens to his camera and had removed it from the tripod. The camera was suspended from a leather strap around his neck and his hands were clasped behind his back. He looked like a soldier at ease. But I knew what he was going to do. He was going to photograph the particularly gnarled parts of the trees where the branches bent in peculiar directions. He had always been very interested in detail. Once he had even shot a series of hotel curtains up close – so that you could see the differences.

'This is impossible,' I said as he wandered around clicking the camera. Then I crumpled up my piece of scrap paper and threw it in one of the metal wastebaskets.

'What was that?' he asked absently.

'A telephone number,' I answered. I wasn't exactly lying. There was a telephone number on that scrap of paper, on the other side. I had no idea whose.

The sun got lower. We began walking again towards the end of town.

'I like this kind of late afternoon light,' he said. 'It picks out detail, intensifies colour.'

I looked down at my shoes which seemed a little intensified, then back at my shadow, which seemed the same, except that it was longer.

'Not too much detail in a shadow,' I commented.

'No,' he agreed.

I began to feel even hungrier than I had in the hotel room and remembered another kind of plate that they sometimes had in restaurants, besides the ones with flowers or the ones with the peacocks. These were usually white and had a picture of the hotel on them along with its name. I was trying to remember whether the picture was sketched in black or grey and finally decided that it was probably black in the original but had turned to grey because people had dragged knives and forks across it year after year. This could happen to any picture on any plate. I'd noticed otherwise normal peacocks with their heads or tails worn away or flowers without petals, but I'd never really thought about it until now.

'Notice how the light picks out the detail on that wall,' he was saying. 'Makes it almost linear. It's only in this kind of light,' he went on, 'that even moss can throw a shadow.' He set up his tripod again, preparing to photograph the shadows of lichen.

What kind of light do they have in hotel restaurants, I wondered. I couldn't remember ever seeing a shadow there. And yet they were filled with waiters, tables, chairs, clients; perpendicular forms quite capable of making shadows. Still, I'd never noticed any. And the food, as far as I could remember, never cast a shadow on the china. I turned so that mine was in front of me, so that it bent when it reached the wall. Then I turned again so that I could see the very end of town and my shadow was behind me once again.

At the end of the town something was blinking and flashing. At first, because I thought it was an accident, I began to anticipate sirens. But then, as I looked harder, shading the sun from my eyes, I discovered that it was simply a merry-go-round. Part of neither a carnival nor a fair; it was all by itself, occupying a vacant lot, just after the architecture stopped and just before the flat expanse of fields began. The lights were to attract attention, to make it seem more important than it was, and to cause people as far away as myself to notice it.

'When you're finished,' I said, 'let's go down there, down to the merry-go-round.'

'Is there one?' he asked, changing lenses again. 'Why don't *you* go down there? And then, by the time you come back up here I'll be finished.' He focused on the moss. 'This light, you see, is absolutely perfect here right now.'

I walked right across the area that the blue workman had been raking, leaving my footprints there. Soon I could distinguish the music that was being played while the merry-go-round went round and round. It was American rock and roll recorded by a French group who obviously didn't understand the lyrics but who liked the melody anyway. *Won't you come out, won't you come out tonight,* they sang. As I got closer I could see that several of the horses were unoccupied, as were two miniature chariots. A group of three or four children stood off to one side eating pink candy floss and waiting for the next ride so that they could climb on board. Their mothers gossiped in another group a few feet away. Directly behind them a brightly painted truck was parked, evidence that this was not a permanent merry-go-round, but one that would, more than likely, move on to another town the following morning.

The day the merry-go-round came to town, I said aloud to myself as I watched the magenta, fuchsia and lime-green lights flash on and off under a bright blue sky. The phrase, I decided, sounded like the beginning of a children's story about skipping school or running away from home. One with gypsies and caravans and babies being born in trunks, where one day you're at a plain brown desk and the next you're walking a tightrope. I would have told him all this if he had been there with me. But he might have stopped me. It might have been the beginning of another accusing monologue.

There I was, right at the end of town, standing in front of a tacky little merry-go-round that was singing *it will be all right if you just come out tonight* in a thick French accent, Dayglo horses going up and down, round and round. I watched and listened until the perfect light abruptly disappeared behind a totally unexpected bank of black, black clouds which had moved, like a dangerous monologue, over the rim of the horizon.

When I turned to walk back up the boulevard I had something else to say out loud to myself. *Merry-go-round,* I whispered, *with approaching storm.*

I was beginning to feel faint with hunger.

SURPRISINGLY, the plates in the restaurant had nothing on them at all except food. Still, as you finished each course you could see the tiny etched lines that had been made, over the years, by people moving knives and forks. We had leek soup, followed by *escargots* and were now working our way through *veau à la crème*. The pangs in my stomach had subsided and the wine was making me want to talk.

'It would have made a good photo,' I said, 'that merry-go-round with that horrible black cloud behind it. And if only you could have got the music too, it would have been terrific.'

'The trouble is,' he said, 'the merry-go-round would have just looked like a merry-go-round with a big black cloud behind it; it wouldn't have looked like anything else.'

'No,' I agreed, 'I guess it wouldn't.'

The pastry cart arrived. We each chose something different so that we could compare and contrast. The light sugary texture was a shock to the palate after the richness of the veal.

Suddenly every single light went out, all over the restaurant.

'It's only the storm,' he explained from somewhere on the other side of the table.

I just went on eating. Eating and eating in the dark.

Bossu

LUST

WHEN HE WAS A CHILD his mother must have warmed his flesh in flannel, pressed his mouth to her breast. At that time his skin might have spread smoothly enough over his frame to camouflage his deformity. And because he had not yet learned to walk, he would be unaware that the burden of it would be his to carry, like permanent baggage, forever. Since then, no one could have touched this enormous, bent man who passes, every day, on the street beyond my windows. The surface of his body has been free of contact. Neither handshake nor embrace has visited the crooked landscape of its vast geography. His sweat and his heat have always been his own.

I have chosen my exile in a foreign village; a place where, knowing little of the language, I'm unable to eavesdrop on the lives of my neighbours. I have brought my anonymity here. He stumbles into my self-absorption, collides with my neutrality. And never knows it. Passing me, passing me by.

At night, when the villagers turn their lights out, an absolute darkness fills the air. The atmosphere becomes so thick I want to claw my way through it towards some sparkling surface. So I often move out to the stars at night, let them buzz in my brain until I grow dizzy, my lungs filled with black air and I stagger up the stone stairs to my bed. There I can close my eyes and bring the constellations back to me, allowing my bloodstream to fill with glitter.

Often I've imagined him sitting, alone, on some iron balcony, large and covered in black, almost blending with the night, except for the white of his face, his hands. On his lap he holds a mirror where he can see the stars – my bloodstream – in the sky. The image is framed in glass. Trapped, touchable. The buzz that fills his mind comes from my brain.

I did not know the language well enough to ask about him. The villagers seem to accept him as part of the fabric of the town. They even nod and say *Bonjour, monsieur* to his down-

cast face. He shuffles on, perhaps not hearing, perhaps not caring. Dogs, however, are disturbed by his presence. They cannot accept this irregularity, this deviation. Each day their furious barking announces his arrival in the streets. He uses his
stick in a vain attempt to disperse them. They travel around
him in circles, barking and snapping. The mothers among
them are particularly avid. Their teats swing as a result of exces-
sive activity.

And he goes by, surrounded by this crazy chorus and the
soft angry drone of his own voice, which *I* know is cursing
both the dogs at his trousers and the street that moves like a
slow conveyor belt under his feet. I swear his brain cracks like a
whip over his body, just to move it one more inch. And I sit
here, behind window glass, *my* brain sniffing around his ankles.

By the time I'd been here three months I knew something of
his routine. He passed my windows every afternoon at two,
returned at three. He was making his way to the monastery at
the end of the street for afternoon mass. I moved my chair and
desk closer to the window in order to be able to observe him.
Now I can sense his arrival without dogs, without bells or
wristwatches. His approach and his withdrawal have become
more predictable than the daily performance of the sun. I know
them as I know my own pulse.

I remember the first time that I saw him. A large dark cloud
had broken at my arrival in this village, my first glimpse of this
house. I was leaning from a window in the rain, opening the
shutters, when he interrupted my view of the neighbour's
dooryard dahlias. He was a huge, moveable monument aching
under an umbrella, a solid block of fear inching down the
street. I saw him as an omen – the first view from my windows
a large hunchback struggling past old stones, dogs snapping at
his heels, his pulpy, white hands clenched. He was entirely
absorbed by his journey over paving stones. From where I
stood I could have touched him. But I knew he didn't notice
me at all.

Immediately, I tried to make use of him as a metaphor, to
create verses with crippled themes. I could only swallow him,
at that point whole, make him part of my own experience. As if
he had no other function than to serve as a convenient image

flung arbitrarily down on my doorstep. I could neither describe nor determine the extent of his own difficulty, wrote self-conscious lines;

like a large hunchback
I carry my pain without grace

until I knew I had no pain and began, in my own way, to create some.

As the days grew shorter I began to search my skin for imperfections, focusing for hours at a time on scars and blemishes. When these no longer pleased me I rubbed dirt into the pores on my face and cultivated the black hair under my arms and on my legs. Finding shears housed in the courtyard potting shed I cropped the long hair on my head as close to the scalp as possible. I fasted much, slept little. Dark circles grew under my eyes, lines adorned my cheeks and forehead. Burdened by desire, fatigue, and hunger my body developed a slight stoop. And, at last, to my great satisfaction, I began to limp.

By the time the village had pulled itself inward for the winter he had become a fact to me: cumbersome, slow-moving, ever present in my thoughts. I whispered the French name 'Bossu' in all of our imaginary conversations. Now I spent my days beside the window (his window), even ate my frugal meals there, hoping to perceive a break in the rhythm of his day, an advance at other than the usual time. I was waiting for a meteor; the star that would escape beyond the edge of his mirror, forcing him to turn his head to follow it. Forcing him to turn his face to me.

One morning I left the comfort of the fire to walk his route around the town, to see the world as he might. Like a child looking for coins another might have lost I kept my eyes down. The curve of each street became the curve of the earth where rivers rushed through gutters towards some magic destination. Brown leaves scraped over cobblestones. Puddles reflected broken pieces of the sky; the clouds, the blue, he'd never actually seen. Eventually I found his voice in the tactile surface of the ground.

That's when I began to prepare for him; subtly at first, but later with more determination. Dressed in the stone colours, the earth colours of the street, my clothes oily and spotted and much too large for me, I approach the window daily. Sometimes I pin thorns and twigs and burrs in my sparse hair. Sometimes I paste muddy leaves to my clothes and stomach. I stand in the light that penetrates the glass, ready for his glance. He doesn't notice me at all.

Despite this, I live a waking dream of him. His name, 'Bossu,' sticks in my throat, its taste on my tongue long into the night. It is the transparent burn left by starbathing on the skin, that black curve of sky, the need for suffocating dark. I want to be the comet that bursts across his brain; the recognition and the fear of his own history.

The shame of it. Standing here by the window dressed for love, my nails against the glass. And he won't notice me at all. He is so involved in the terrible suffering of just getting there, his survival ignores my silent call. He simply cannot stop to answer it. No gesture, no transformation can disturb the burden of his flesh as he moves beneath it. Passing me by.

But later tonight, when I leave the house to move out to the stars, the dogs will be waiting in the darkness, just beyond my doorway.

Her Golden Curls

ENVY

AMY JEFFERSON had seven different dresses, all with puffed sleeves, each a different pastel shade. She had a dog called Rags who was smaller than most farm dogs and who was allowed to sleep, like a soft round pillow, on the parlour furniture. She had boots made of Spanish leather and four china dolls. When she described her room to me I associated it with birthday cake. There were, she said, pink quilts, satin pillows, muslin curtains and a dressing table trimmed with eyelet lace. And it was her room. She had no brothers or sisters with whom she might have had to share.

We were both eight years old. The road from her farm to ours was fourteen miles long. A great distance. But not for Amy Jefferson who arrived in her father's motor car, her lovely dress covered with a fine powder of dust from the road. My mother would run to get the clothes brush for Amy and my sisters would run to the drive to get a better look at the motor car. My father, prouder, would attempt to discuss crops with Amy's father while he secretly eyed the wealthier man's glorious machine.

Amy and I were to play, but it seemed that we never did much of that. Sometimes we fooled around with an incomplete deck of cards that were kept in the kitchen drawer. Occasionally we threw a ball back and forth in the yard. But mostly those afternoons were spent as a kind of inquisition on my part and a kind of confession on hers. I barely gave her time to answer one question before I moved on to the next. *Please tell me again about the big doll, the one from France,* or *Does your bed really have a mauve satin comforter as well as a pink spread? Have you really been to the National Exhibition and did you go there in the motor car? Do you have books with coloured pictures? How many toys do you have that move by themselves?* I don't know whether I loved her or hated her, whether I was pleased or enraged by her answers. I only know that Amy Jefferson and her possessions became a kind of addiction for me. And even though I was angered by my sisters' accusations (*Trevor has a girlfriend*), I simply couldn't get enough.

It was as though that summer had *become* Amy Jefferson. When she was not there, the details that made up the fabric of experience seemed to be missing as well. I would pass the days between her visits lying on the grass watching cumulus clouds move across the sky. Even they were connected to Amy Jefferson, assuming the shapes of her worldly goods; satin bows and puffed sleeves, beautiful, unobtainable clothing fourteen miles beyond my grasp. Sometimes Amy Jefferson's satin comforter sailed by or one of her muslin curtains. Once I even thought I saw Rags up there, though at the time I had absolutely no idea what he looked like. Once I thought I saw Amy herself with her long golden hair, stretched out by wind, across the sky.

Amy Jefferson's mother was dead; something I found quite horrifying yet vaguely appealing at the same time. This meant that Amy's home was equipped with a housekeeper whose main function was to look after the motherless little girl (iron her pretty dresses, make her down-filled bed). And, of course, her father doted on her, called her his *princess* or *my little lady*. He read to her from all those books with the coloured pictures, and he took her for hundreds of rides in the motor car, even allowing her to honk the alarming horn.

I, on the other hand, was looked after by several females whose attentions were affectionate but terse. Until Amy, I'd never really felt there was any room for complaint. But now when my mother filled my dresser drawers with drab corduroys and denims or when my oldest sister announced that it was evident that my hair needed cutting, I felt there was an edge of cruelty to their actions and remarks. They seemed to be deliberately shutting me out of Amy's world: a world of colour and comfort, a world of personal and environmental beauty.

Amy was a first-class narrator and it wasn't long before she decided to tell me, in detail, her version of her mother's death. Old Man Cassidy, she assured me, had stuffed her mother in a garbage pail and had taken her away to die. *Who,* I asked, was this awful person? Amy explained that Old Man Cassidy was a wizard tramp. No one had ever seen him but he lived up in the hills behind Jeffersons' farm. He had evil magic powers and for years had envied Amy's mother's golden hair. He had killed her, therefore, for no other reason than to steal her blond curls which he now wore *on his own head*. When asked how she discovered this Amy replied that she just *knew*, and that was all there was to that. Then she chanted a song, like the kind girls skip to, making the incident vividly clear in my imagination:

> *'Old Man Cassidy's a mean old man*
> *Stuffed my mother in a garbage can*
> *Took her to his shack*
> *And cut off all her hair*
> *And wrapped her up like garbage*
> *And threw her down the stairs.'*

It never occurred to me to doubt the existence of such a terrifying individual. The mental image that the story, and subsequent song, conjured up was instant and precise. From that day on my nightmares included a gnarled old man dressed in tattered clothing with golden curls cascading down his back. I had no trouble imagining the hair, since, once a week, I saw some just like it tumbling out from underneath Amy Jefferson's straw sunhat.

After three or four visits I persuaded Amy to bring along some of her picture books. In these slender volumes, for the first time, I saw actual representations of the stories I had been told by my mother and sister, stories in which terrible things happened to beautiful women. At best, it appeared that they were made to scrub floors for indefinite periods of time. At worst, they were given poisoned apples to eat so that they would sleep for centuries inside glass coffins, eventually to be rescued by ineffectual, anemic-looking princes. In my imagination I cast Amy in the role of the beautiful women, and myself, if only by reason of my sex, in the role of the princes. Then I envied her more interesting, if more dangerous part.

By August the first bright green of summer had begun to fade and the earth on our drive was baked hard by the sun. Amy and I picked huge extravagant bouquets of golden rod for my mother, who immediately banished them from the kitchen because of my older sister's hay fever. My father embarrassed my by suggesting we ride one of the gentle old workhorses when I knew that Amy had a perfectly beautiful pony at home who would make Bessie look clumsy and stupid by comparison. We talked a little more about 'Old Man Cassidy,' speculating about what terrible crime he might commit next. Most often, however, we played a game invented by me as a result of the picture books, a game called *The Prince and the Beauty*. During the course of this entertainment I got to kiss Amy on the lips in order to awaken her from whatever length of poisoned sleep we had previously arranged. Once I suggested that we switch roles, that maybe occasionally I could be the Beauty. Amy quickly squashed that idea. I was a boy, she said, and nobody ever gave poisoned apples to boys. Besides, I didn't have the golden curls necessary to qualify as a Beauty. She would, however, allow me to be Old Man Cassidy, who was, more often than not, responsible for the evil fruit.

Near the end of summer, Amy's weekly visits abruptly stopped. I asked no questions, assuming her absence was the result of some adult decision over which I had no control. Besides, my sisters had spied on one of our extended entertainments, had seen the kissing part, and had given me no peace since. And so, released from the responsibilities of playing both the good and evil male, and the longing for a little girl's possessions that her presence induced, I was vaguely relieved by Amy's absence. I reverted to my games with sticks and dust and happily forgot about ribbons and curls. At least for a while.

Then, just when the trees on our lane were beginning to turn, my father received a letter that caused a great stir in the kitchen. When he passed it silently to my mother to read, her eyes opened wide, as if she were greatly surprised. My older sisters gathered round and, having read the contents, fluttered and gasped. Soon they and my mother were busy pulling mixing bowls and baking tins out of the cupboards, while my father explained that the following day we were all to visit the Jeffersons' farm.

This, I knew, was to be an important event. A party, no doubt, in Amy's honour. I could scarcely sit still at the dinner table, squirmed in pure joy for several minutes until I lapsed once again into an attack of raw jealousy. I had never had a party after all, just a cake at supper with my family. And my parents had *never* been this awestruck by any event related to me. Even later that night, after I had gone to bed, I could hear them muttering Amy's name in the kitchen, and that of her father, over and over.

I WAS NOT AT ALL SURPRISED to discover that Amy Jefferson's house was an imposing structure with two porches, one on top of another. The front yard was immense and was bisected by a narrow cement walk edged by two perfectly clipped hedges. These extended to surround most of the lawn, which was itself beautifully mown; Amy Jefferson's farm was equipped with a machine expressly for that purpose. Rising from the grass was a large oak tree and hanging from that a child's swing. For Amy Jefferson's private amusement.

At the side of the house, beyond the small walls of the hedgerows, a number of women were gathered. They were placing white tablecloths on wooden tables. It was a breezy day, which made their activities difficult, and four women were required to cover one table – two to shake the cloth, brilliant in the sun, out into the wind, two more to catch the flapping corners on the opposite side. Dressed in the long, dark skirts of the period, these women looked like black shadows dancing slow upon the lawn, unfurling white banners, serious and quiet at their task. I envied Amy Jefferson these shadows who were so obviously dedicated to her pleasure.

We entered the kitchen and deposited there the food that my mother and sisters had spent the previous evening preparing. But the wealth of edibles already there suggested that they need not have bothered. More dark-skirted women drifted silently around the table, moving dishes to make room for the baked goods we had brought. We stood uncomfortably to one side until one of the women, who identified herself as the housekeeper, asked if we would like to see Amy and led us down a long hall, with remarkably polished floors, and into the parlour where a large number of adults were collected in a murmuring crowd.

Once inside this room my parents shook off their hesitation and seemed to know exactly what to do. They took hold of me, each by one hand, and walked towards the opposite side of the room. I remember looking down, envying Amy Jefferson the colours on her parlour carpet. Then I remember being lifted up by my father to be presented with the white face and still body of Amy herself. She was dressed in pink, her puffed sleeves crushed against the mauve satin of the coffin's interior, her golden curls motionless against her chest. Her skin looked smooth and hard, like porcelain. She resembled a china doll.

'Kiss her,' my mother said.

THE AFTERNOON PASSED like an Indian summer dream. Tens of wagons journeyed out to a cemetery where they put Amy in the ground; satin, puffed sleeves and curls, down into damp and dark. And we returned to the lawn where the dark-skirted ladies tempted me with cakes and said what a nice little boy I was. Cumulus clouds carried the ghosts of Amy's possessions over the crowd of adult mourners, who murmured and shook their heads and ate all of the food that had covered the kitchen table. Rags appeared and was fed table scraps. Amy's swing moved back and forth in a warm wind.

When it was all over and we were about to leave I noticed Amy's father standing apart from his guests, looking off in the distance towards the woods at the back of his farm. His face was immobile but his eyes were like clenched fists. I suspected that his mind at that moment was filled with the image of an old, old man, dressed in the costume of a tramp, with enough blond curls on his shoulders for two good-sized wigs. I was amazed and relieved by his apparent naivety. For I knew whose sinful longings had sucked the life out of his treasured victim. I presumed that my envy and obsession had weakened and destroyed Amy as surely as any poisoned apple. I turned and was horribly sick as a result of all the sweets I had eaten at the large white table, and the half-hour spent afterwards playing on Amy Jefferson's private swing.

All the way home I examined the texture of my own short hair, expecting that, at any minute, the blond curls of my guilt might come into evidence all over my head.

The Boat

PRIDE

THE CHILDREN spotted it first and simply watched it in an attitude children will take – plastic pails hanging, forgotten, from their hands, muscles tensed, alert. It looked to them like a wounded sea monster, thrashing and lurching in the waves. But when it moved closer and they saw it was a boat, they ran to us in great excitement. For although impressive yachts and sleek fibreglass sail-boats floated through their days at the beach, this craft, coming as it so obviously did from somewhere else, and heading for their very own shore, seemed to them to be the essence of what a boat should be.

I sat in my deck-chair under a colourful umbrella, reading the paper and staring at the ocean. My wife knitted. We seldom spoke, except to the grandchildren. To call them back in concern, to tie hats firmly on small heads to prevent sunstroke, or to apply more sun-tan lotion. I was golden brown and quite fat. I looked vaguely tired in the manner of older people who are only halfway through the two-week visit with children of whom they are overly fond. My wife had brought a picnic lunch with her to the beach and she was thinking about that now – the small problems associated with eating there: keeping the grandchildren from eating too fast, or from eating nothing but chips and cookies, or from eating too much sand. The appearance of the boat interrupted her midday thoughts as even she shaded her eyes to determine the nature of the distressed vessel.

Its mast, which I would later come to know was made from the trunk of a slender tree, slapped the surface of the water, and then, as if involved in a desperate struggle, hauled itself upward, totem-like, against the sky. Hanging down from this, attached by a series of disorganized ropes, was a sail of real canvas. Part of it lay crumpled in the interior of the boat, but the major portion was draped over the gunwales and bubbled in the water. Unbleached, the beige colour seemed so unfamiliar, so non-plastic, that in its altered, broken state it was like the ghost of an earlier time and it frightened me somewhat, though I didn't know why.

Having caught the attention of everyone on the beach directly before it, the boat made its limping progress towards the shore. Propelled forward by one six-foot wave, it would pause briefly, rock slightly, and wait for the thrust of the next, moving sometimes sideways, sometimes forward as it was meant to. By now the life-guard, who was posted at our rear, could see through his binoculars that the boat, at one time, had probably belonged to a fisherman and was meant to be managed by a series of large oars. The mast and sail, then, would have had to be a later addition, made for the purpose of moving the boat out of the calm of some harbour and into the thick of an inexplicable journey. He could also see that whoever had planned this journey was absent, as were any passengers, that they had either been rescued at sea, or more likely had been swept overboard by the huge waves that had existed on the ocean for the last few days. Laying down his binoculars on his tanned thighs he relaxed his shoulders feeling functionless in this particular drama.

Within a half an hour the boat had ended its marine performance and had, with one last determined shove, buried its prow in the wet sand at the shoreline. There it rested, listing somewhat to the starboard side, its sail moving back and forth in the water with the motion of the waves. The children ran to it to peer inside. I, too, left my deck-chair, my Styrofoam cooler, my newspaper, to look at what the sea had brought in.

The children, of course, were most interested in the boat as an object. They responded instantly to the brightly coloured boards and twisted ropes. And they especially loved the broken parts of the boat where the flat planks had separated from the frame and tiny waterfalls appeared with each new wave. Small lakes had gathered at the bottom of the hull and beneath the prow was a perfect, enclosed, damp space where several small people might huddle together and giggle. Their hands automatically reached up to the gunwales in their desire to climb inside, to claim the boat as their own.

But I held them back. Sensing the blacker side, I knew that

the boat called to my mind something I had forgotten so completely that I could not remember it even now with the fact of it rolling there in front of me at the edge of the ocean. And when I saw the open suitcase, the clothing, the portable baby's bed, the toothbrush, the shoes, all of which littered the hull, I understood that whoever had set out to sea in such a craft had arrived in my world despite rescue or death.

The life-guard and I hauled the boat farther up onto the beach, beyond the tide line. Then, standing slightly back, we began to speculate about its origins. The astonishing lack of synthetic fibre suggested to us that the boat was most certainly foreign. I thought it might have come from one of the smaller, more obscure Caribbean islands. He suggested South America. Our conversation dwindled. It seemed futile to discuss the fate of the boat's passengers, or even their reason for attempting to cross the sea in such a dangerous fashion. So we stood back and looked, our arms folded, feeling cheated, a bit, of the sensationalism that so often accompanies accidental death in our own country.

THAT NIGHT, tucked snugly away in our climate-controlled condominium, I dreamt a hundred dreams of the boat. In one dream I was building the boat, or at least working on part of it. Sometimes I pushed large sharp needles through tough canvas. Sometimes I wove ropes. In some far corner of my brain, where I remembered my father's carpentry shop, I steamed and bent wood for the frame long into the night. Then I fitted the skeleton-like construction together in record time. My mother, whom I had all but forgotten, appeared in one of the dreams, saying over and over in a carping, critical fashion, 'It looks like the ribcage of a dead elephant. It looks like the ribcage of a dead elephant,' until I shouted at her, in a way I never would have done in real life, 'Well, *you* are elephant flesh; grey, loose and wrinkling!' Then I dreamt I was planking the frame – setting the thin bevelled boards higher and higher, fastening them with bright galvanized nails. I whispered to myself in an unfamiliar language. 'Garboard, shutter, sheerstake,' I said quietly, but with amazing confidence. The work went well.

My wife, because she had been a mother, dreamt about

mending the boat – caulking the seams with cotton dresses she had thrown away years before and patching the holes with oil-cloth and horse-hoof glue. She claimed she spent half the night untying the knots in the ropes and winding them up into well-organized, tidy coils. Then she carefully stitched the torn sail, sometimes with brightly coloured embroidery thread, some-times with the more functional white variety. Later she repainted the simple geometric design, which had, in some places, been rubbed off the stern. And finally, she dreamt that she hauled the sail away from the place where it lay in the damp sand, put it through the wash cycle in an enormous machine, and hung it out to dry on a clothes-line strung between two telephone poles. And all the Lincolns, Chryslers and Cadillacs on Ocean Boulevard ground to a halt, amazed to see this expanse of canvas, like a brown flag with grommets, flap up towards the sky.

The children dreamt of sailing the boat, or of driving it, or flying it, depending on their personalities, just as it was – injured, wrecked – with sand and water spilling into its hull and its sail dragging behind it like long drowned hair. They were too young, too satisfied, to actively search for change in their dreams and so they dreamt of the fact of the boat and of access to that fact; of scaling the sides, leaping over the gun-wales and sitting at the rudderless helm. In truth they dreamt of taking command of the boat as something the sea had arbi-trarily given them.

WHEN WE ARRIVED at the beach the following morning the boat looked more familiar, less foreign to us. I brought my little black camera with me and marched down the beach with it to capture the image of the boat from all sides, forever. My wife fussed and clucked, almost affectionately, about the untidiness of the boat. Some of the clothing, which had earlier spilled from the hull, had been brought in by the waves and had formed a colourful strip at the tide line. She moved slowly towards this and, gingerly picking up the pieces of fabric, dropped them in a neat pile, hoping that the machine that came at night to bury seaweed would dispose, as well, of this reminder of the human factor.

The children began to play with the portable baby's bed.

Unnoticed behind the stern they constructed a sail from a large stick and a plaid cotton shirt. Borrowing the laces from an unmatched shoe that hung from the port gunwale, they were able to tie miniature ropes through the buttonholes and pull the fabric tight enough to catch the wind. They pounded the stick through the canvas bottom of the tiny bed and placed the youngest child inside as a navigator. Then, screaming with joy, they propelled their little craft out to sea where it turned slowly round a few times before being pushed under by the white froth of an incoming wave.

So all that day my stock market quotations and the children's plastic pails lay untouched in the sand beside the deck-chairs as we all responded to the boat. Sometimes we just stood and stared at it. It was something that could not be interpreted but could not be turned away from either. Sometimes we commented to each other that it really was a strong boat and might, in fact, be made seaworthy once again. The children played around the edges of the boat, having been forbidden, since the incident of the baby's bed, to touch either the vessel or its contents.

ON THE SECOND NIGHT the dreams revisited us but in slightly different form. I, for instance, dreamt that I had discovered a miniature model of the boat. Walking through the streets of an unfamiliar city I had seen it in a junk shop window and had decided to purchase it though the price was much too high. When I placed it on the mantelpiece in my living-room, my wife had demanded: 'Who told you I wanted a family portrait over the fireplace?' and I had replied, 'You'll never know till you light the fire.' I awakened with my heart pounding to discover that my wife, in the twin bed opposite, had been dreaming of adopting a child from a small obscure Caribbean island.

But before this she dreamed of her childhood home, which had miraculously evolved into the boat. Upside down, the keel had become the peak of the roof, and, with little alteration, planks had turned to clapboard. Inside, the windows were gaping holes, providing a variety of ocean views and covered with curtains made of torn clothing and shoe laces. Her father crouched in the left-hand corner of the overturned stern, reading the Bible and writing stock market quotations in the damp sand of the floor. When we went back to sleep I dreamed I was a fisherman considering immigration to a new land.

One of the children dreamed that he could see the pattern of the boat clearly charted by stars in a navy-blue sky. It was situated right between the Big and Little Dippers. He pointed it out to a crowd that had assembled somewhere vaguely to his left but they had been unable to see even the Big or Little Dipper and spoke only of fireflies and satellites.

The next day we were all easy with the boat, as if our vision of the beach had expanded just enough to include it. And so, when late in the morning we watched the uniformed men tie the boat to their own authoritative coast guard vessel, we felt remotely sad and guilty too, as if the boat had committed some obscure crime, to which we were a party. We asked and were told that the boat would be filled with weights and sunk at sea. Our last glimpse of it was a spot of red on the horizon – its painted stern glowing in the sun.

The following week vacation ended and the children returned to their home in the north where winter gradually bleached their brown skins. When they spoke of the boat, they did so with such confusion that their mother assumed that they had been taken on a fishing excursion, and their father believed that they had been presented with an expensive toy by us, their over-indulgent grandparents. Even their drawings, which often included the boat, were quickly glanced at by their parents and then forgotten.

We quickly readjusted to our childless existence and finally forgot about the boat altogether except when it entered our unremembered dreams. Each day we went to the beach and sat beneath our colourful umbrellas. My wife knitted. We seldom spoke. I read stock-market quotations. She unpacked the Styrofoam cooler. Sleek fibreglass sail-boats and impressive yachts sailed across our constant vision of the sea. And when, a month later, our attention focused on the horizon, we did not recognize the subject of our dreams, the object of our very own design, believing instead that it was merely a wounded sea monster, thrashing and lurching in the waves. But the children had gone. This time we had caused the image, created it. This time it was our unsubstantial pride, moving slowly, painfully back to shore.

Artificial Ice

ANGER

EVERY NIGHT I danced *La Sylphide,* creating my reputation with them as 'the daughter of the air.' Heavy blue curtains opened and closed on fantasy after fantasy – painted scenery, paper gold. But I knew the blocks of wood inside my shoes, the hard reality of the boards beneath my feet. I knew no sylph with wings could lure a man from his marriage – the cold porridge of his life. I had spoken to myself about it often. No man, I said, will break through the walls he has built for a woman who flies, whether her flight be caused by magic, or, as in my case, by days of sweat in front of a ruthless mirror. And I continued to know this even on the nights when my dressing-room filled with white roses, champagne, diamonds.

But that night, my costume was new, with real silver threads woven through the cloth. These are the trails of meteors, my dressmaker said, running her hands across the glitter. And she was right. Dressed in it I scarcely touched the ground, burned across the stage. And later I received my encores and my roses with grace, felt, for the first time, a stirring of affection towards the audience, that anonymous beast whose eyes had scrutinized my flesh. So that even when I discovered darker roses (blood inside my shoes), I was not distracted from the exceptional mood of the performance.

They were a people dominated by weather, held in check by unceasing cold. An irremovable layer of frost covered their windows in early October, cancelling all hope of a view for months to come. Icicles hung heavy on the beards of the men and snow filled the children's hair. I was told of women from the rural areas who grew fingernails of ice, which hardened to such a degree that they never melted, even when their hands reached for flowers during that brief season. The dogs and horses that I saw had eyes with crystal retinas and coats covered with layers of hoar-frost. By January each year a solid stillness had entered the air. Too cold for snow, a final terrifying freeze set in and the outdoors became, in fact, quite dangerous. The lungs of a newborn baby could petrify in a second. A tear could solidify and leave serious scratches on an eyeball.

Adults adjusted, however, to this prolonged winter and went about their business in the streets taking shallow well-ordered breaths and wearing a special kind of mask that was said to prevent damage to the eyes. But there was a further problem. The extra heat and moisture caused by the vibrations of vocal cords caused spoken words to crystallize and fall to the ground, replacing the discontinued snow. Occasionally, therefore, you would see a tiny set of white hills and know that there had been a conversation. In fact, in their language, the word *conversation* referred both to the familiar interchange of words and the tiny mounds of snow left on the street afterwards. And sometimes these, combined with identifiable footprints, could be used as evidence of one sort or another; evidence that, in some cases, was more precise and more meaningful than fingerprints. During the long ten months of their winter, therefore, the people seldom spoke.

But they responded with unusual enthusiasm to gesture, and passionately loved the dance. Each night the huge theatre, situated in the city's centre, was filled to capacity with a silent, attentive crowd. The women dressed in white satin and diamonds to match their national season. Over their heads the magnificent crystal chandeliers were scarcely warmed by the thousands of candles that burned in them. Above these were ceiling frescos of blue and silver and below a grey carpet like the first thickness of ice that covered the river early in autumn. And then the men, dressed in soft mauve uniforms, their pale blue eyes fixed on my darker, unfamiliar skin, night after night.

Their prince, well acquainted with the ballets of the time, had followed my career for a long time before he sent for me to come and dance in his country. He heated the theatre, especially for me, with four giant furnaces and provided me with a coach to travel in. I was also given a house five miles from the city limits, where blue-grey ice stretched out towards infinity. Here messengers skated to my door with gifts from the palace: wonderful furs and velvets, and quantities of jewels – diamonds, sapphires, pearls. But the prince never appeared in my rooms, preferring, perhaps, to arouse my curiosity by the strange visual messages he sometimes sent along with the gifts. I would pull from envelopes a variety of objects masquerading as letters: a handful of frozen tears; a delicate bracelet made entirely of ice, which melted on my wrist; his fingerprints pressed into white wax; and once, a bright blue heart painted on the inside of the wrapper of a razor blade.

The thought of him, this elusive prince, began to fill my waking hours. The first thing I would see each morning, when I breathed on the frost that covered the window pane, was his messenger's skate blades gleaming on the horizon. They were like razors reflecting the sun. I spent my leisure hours inventing the pretty words I was certain he would say to me, imagining caresses. Someone said he kept a tiny room filled with photographs of me. Someone else said that he had demanded that all the ribbons from my discarded shoes be sent to him. I was fascinated. I desperately wanted to see him. I arranged elaborate dinners, unusual concerts at my house, hoping he would appear. I sent him special invitations scented with spices. He was utterly unyielding.

Eventually I soothed myself by sending him small objects as a kind of reply to his constant messages: a starfish from my warm native sea, three of my dark eyelashes, and finally one of my shoes, filled with the blood of the previous evening's performance. I knew that by the time it reached him, travelling through the freeze in the messenger's pocket, the liquid would be frozen – a ruby of sorts – some real colour in exchange for the silver of the jewels and the pure white of his absence.

After that we spoke once, outside the door that was my entrance to the theatre. He asked if I was pleased with my surroundings, with the servants, the furs, the jewels, whether the music was correct, too fast, too slow, whether my supply of shoes was sufficient, my dressmaker adequate. Answering his questions I examined his eyes, so amazingly pale. But some flame was there, the edge of the fire at night, cold blue. Heat disguised as ice.

Later, when all was black beyond the edges of the stage, I thought I saw the silver braid of his uniform, shining like a skate blade from the depths of the theatre. Me dancing *La Sylphide,* becoming for his country 'the daughter of the air,' his obsession and then his indifference around me like blue

peripheral light. When I left the theatre I saw the two miniature mountains of our only conversation standing side by side
with our footprints behind them, his static, mine restless and
confused. I laughed aloud in the presence of such meaningless
evidence.

My dressmaker was enthralled by my black hair. She said it
shone like the wings of blackbirds and made her sad since the
presence of any bird was brief in that country unless it was
caged and forced to sing in some rich woman's boudoir. And I
said that I'd always wanted hair like corn silk, like spun silver.
Then she promised me the costume I wore that evening, silver
threads as fine as hair, running through the gauze. After the
performance I refused to remove it, wore it under fur to my
coach, to the journey that I made each night, five miles over ice
to my house.

Travelling, I could hear the icicle beard of the driver clattering in the wind. When the light inside the carriage changed I
knew we had left the city. I had never seen the winter landscape
at night. Breathe though I might on the windows of the coach,
the frost was too thick to be penetrated. This night, however,
the light of the city was replaced by a colder, bluer illumina-
tion, and I knew there was a moon. My small stove threw shadows on the interior of the coach, the empty plush seat across
from me. Exhausted from the performance, lulled by the
motions of travel, I fell into a deep sleep.

And dreamed my special coloured dreams of flying. Landscape, southern and lush, passing beneath me with such clarity
I could see each pebble at the bottom of the sea as I followed
the coast. Poppies, red and yellow, grew on the edges of highways, wisteria in full bloom over doorways. Dark pines,
cypresses reaching up towards my arms, soft curve of hills, the
gentle herds of animals. And my dancer's shadow down there,
created by sun, fluctuating with each change of elevation.

I awakened to an utterly opposite geography. The coach had
stopped and its door was flung open to endless snow, sharp
stars, moon and velvet sky. Imprinted on this, darker than the
rest, was the figure of a man who, masked and covered by a
long cloak, had, at last, responded to my invitations.

The driver, immobilized by fear at the sight of the pistol,
said nothing. And the man behind the mask filled up the night

with his silence. But when he placed the skin of an animal on the snow and turned to remount his horse, I understood that he wanted a solitary performance, wanted me to dance, for him, alone, in a frozen, anonymous landscape, where no trace of evidence could possibly survive. The pistol shone, like a final denial, in his hand.

When I began to dance, I danced towards the heavens, that whirling vortex, an extension of my costume stretched across the sky. I danced and hardly touched the skin beneath my shoes. Black music, blue music, then silver in my ears. And then the music of the moon, transparent and frightening, like the hot steam of his breath against the cold. Sweat crystallized along my inner arms, my bare thighs, until frost covered my body like fine down. Once the moonlight shone on his exposed teeth where he carried either a grimace or a smile, and once on the ice-blue edge of fire in his eyes. As I reached for something in the sky and was finished, a handful of diamonds landed at my feet. And then my private music was broken apart, into the sound of his moving away.

I RETURNED to the south with jewels in my luggage and anger lodged like glass inside the network of my veins. When I dance now in my own country they call me the daughter of the earth. My costumes are crimson and yellow; passion and anger are in my gestures. The anger is the window that I look through to the world. It is what I eat and what I dream and what I dance. I keep it close to me always for clarity. It is the source of my energy, the root of my self.

And, now when I open the drawer that holds them, the diamonds look like artificial ice among the other stones of blue and white. Even this hot anger could never melt their cold, which is clean and exact and permanent. And speaking deep within their icy centre is the blue flame of his eyes. Here, inside this drawer, where I keep loose fragments of that time: the night sky, pain and frozen stars, the joy and then the anger, the terrifying love he never felt for me. All of this, locked and unlocked by the key of anger.

Ice and sapphires.

Ice and pearls.

Venetian Glass

COVETOUSNESS

I DISCOVERED HER in Florence. Her mother owned a house there to which my companions and I were often invited, as were other grand tourists of the time. This house, I remember, was vast and damp; so damp, in fact, that paint could be peeled from the wall by a careless brush of the sleeve and the books in shelves were warped and covered with mould. The room she entered that first time was lit by a single inadequate fire whose warmth did not extend as far as the furniture. But she, entering, brought heat with her, or so I thought at the time.

She was my first obsession. Quiet and steady, she moved through the rooms of that house carrying silver trays filled with glasses of sherry for her guests. When she passed by the large windows, light reflected from these goblets and shone on the contours of her face, adding an artificial flicker of emotion to a surface that otherwise remained in a state of passive ease.

My tutor was concerned about my response to her and lectured me long into the night. Although he spoke of Raphael or Signorelli, or the faces of Giotto's women, or Botticelli's, I knew it was to distract me from her face, which had begun to shine in my mind like a constant moon. Sometimes he referred to the itinerary we would follow when the winter months were finished, describing the relics we might find along the way: the incorruptible tongue of Saint Anthony in Padua, the bones of the cardinals in the Campo Santo in Pisa. But I knew he was speaking of *my* tongue, *my* bones, warning me of the effects of unprescribed, unpremeditated love.

The object of our journey was twofold, designed for the purpose of furthering my education and in the hope that we might bring back some tangible souvenirs to adorn, temporarily, the walls and shelves of my father's country house, and later, when the plans for my marriage were completed, to permanently adorn mine. And so, when we were not trying to determine the vague shapes of frescos in dark old churches, we were scouring bazaars and shops for treasure. Although my tutor, who had made the tour several times, had a much better eye than mine, neither of us was an expert and we were often mistaken in our purchases. However, I am pleased to report that several of those souvenirs remain with me still: a tiny Sassetta, depicting an obscure saint surrounded by gold leaf, some sections of Roman statuary, which have been authenticated, and Etruscan pottery shards. We picked up other, less notable Italian primitives, some fine silver, and also some wonderful chairs in Naples, for very little cost. My tutor suggested we delay any purchases of lace until we reached Venice, as well as any purchases of glass.

The girl in Florence had finished her education, as much as women ever will, could play the pianoforte, make pictures in watercolour or needlepoint, and write sentimental verse in a clear round hand. She and her mother had lived in Florence for over a year and, as a result, she knew a great deal more than I about the paintings and sculpture there. Yet none of this attracted me to her. It was something in her manner, or something I invented in her manner – a kind of permanent state of grace in my presence, which seemed to grow and substantiate itself as she became less and less a stranger to me. Not that I saw it in her face. Her expression remained unchanged. But I felt, in the air around her, a quivering intensity, like the life and landscape you see trembling on the surface of a pond.

The winter passed in a series of afternoon tea parties and evening dinner parties, either at her house or at the homes of other English in the area. I think of it now as a kind of game. If I laid down the correct cards I was able to sit next to her at the table or better, across from her, to allow my eyes to speak to hers. She was a beauty, no one contested that. Her throat I remember as being particularly fine; and some life pulsed there that I could not quite interpret. This fractional knowledge fascinated me, that and her complete serenity. I wanted the details of her thoughts, wanted to be the man who broke open what I believed to be her camouflage of calm.

As soon as I discovered that she, her mother, and a few companions intended to tour Italy in the summer, I began to arrange my itinerary to coincide with theirs. I was becoming aware, however, that from that point on my actions would have to be subtle. So I decided that I could not appear in each of the towns they planned to visit and when I did appear it would have to seem coincidental. I was a clever young man. I planned my strategy with the knowledge that, in certain circumstances, withdrawal is just as powerful as approach. I knew how to impose my presence so that it would later articulate my absence. To disappear from the room, for example, in the middle of a discussion in which I had played an important role and to which there had not yet been a conclusion. To speak of fictional marvels that I longed to show her in a forthcoming city and then never appear in that city, giving her no directions that she might find these wonders herself. To read a letter in her presence, allowing moods to pass like weather across my face, and then not divulge the contents of that letter. The idea being to create, in a hundred small ways, a void that only increased conversation and contact could fill. So that eventually, in farther foreign places, she would begin to search for me.

And even at that young age, as if by instinct, I knew the effects of place. In Rome I ran to extravagance, entertaining her, and those of her party, at every possible moment, taking them to concerts, plays, fine feasts, making no attempt, at first, to speak to her alone, even though the blood rushed to my head when she turned toward another at the table or sent a quiet smile toward an actor in the *Commedia*.

At last a day arrived when her companions and mine, friendly as a result of the extended contact I had thrust upon them, decided to make an excursion to pay their devotions, such as they were, to the Virgin at Monte de Guardia. She and I stayed behind to visit the church of Santa Maria Maggiore. There, in that strangely columned interior, on those cold and swelling geometric floors, I knew that setting had meshed with purpose and I spoke, for the first time, of my affection for her. I remember church dust catching the hem of her skirt and a shaft of late afternoon sun passing through stained glass and touching her shoulder. And I remember the moment when the serenity of her expression changed, the moment when she opened to me.

My tutor, meanwhile, had not forgotten his employment.

As persistent as a toothache, he was always at my side, tempting me with slightly damaged panel paintings, or worn tapestries, or yellowed ivories from the Middle Ages. But by then my dreams were full of her. Details of her costume occupied my thoughts: the pearl button of her glove, or the violet braid on her skirt. I imagined her in mirrors, plaiting her hair or fixing a cameo in the small hollow between her collar-bones. Moving from the strong sun of Italian noons into the blind dark of churches I felt I was moving into her arms, as if they were as strong and mysterious as this foreign religion we seemed to be constantly invading. Even now, as an old man, when I think of Rome, it appears to me in the form of her pale brow and the puzzled look around her eyes. The shock of this, her first shift from a calm and neutral territory, had stunned her as a blow or sudden loss might have, and I remember her figure, slightly bent under this loss, drifting under dark oil paintings, day after day.

We moved on to Bologna in later spring. It was already dry and hot and dust gathered on eyelashes, her eyelashes. I swear, if I could have seen it all as a reflection in her eyes, I would have been content. But appearances had to be kept up. My tutor, and indirectly my father, had to be appeased. My education had to be furthered. Words like *Gothic* and *Renaissance* had to be stamped into my soul.

She meanwhile held to me. Her presence, as if winged, disturbed the still air. Her body blocked the view, like an Italian portrait where the charming landscape is all but obliterated by the head and shoulders of a countess. I was unable to look past her to the monuments I was expected to remember. In our evening conversations my tutor was appalled by my lack of recall; told me my head was hollow, called me visually illiterate, until I explained that monuments perplexed me – that unless they were smashed into shards they were immovable, incapable of being crated and shipped to England and therefore irrelevant to my future. Unless it carried with it the possibility of possession, no physical object could hold my attention long.

By early June we were in Padua, a city of orange and yellow streets filled with chanting children. Again she and I found ourselves alone in one of those large, cold pieces of religious architecture that were so much a part of our journey. This time it was a pilgrimage place – the Basilica of Saint Anthony. She there in a dress of dark, dark blue, practically blending into the walls except for the moon of her face. The church was no beauty, a jumble of the worst of several periods. Inside this disorder the purity of her form was absolute, gradually reappearing as my eyes adjusted to the darkness. We performed the dance one does in such places: up the centre aisle, down the side aisles, round and round, past all those sombre confessionals where those of the faith describe their sins to a faceless grate. And then we came to the chapel where the treasure of the basilica was housed.

There I stopped, completely overcome by it. There were crowns and chalices of gold inlaid with emeralds and rubies, filigree pendants and fibulas, sceptres and bowls and, most amazing, over one hundred reliquaries besides the one that held the tongue of the departed saint. It was an accumulation of radiance, a concise pageant of glory. I couldn't imagine the hands of craftsmen who could work such miniature miracles. Such accessibility. I wanted to touch it all, to leave my fingerprints as evidence of my desire to possess it, to be in control of it. I wanted to harness the refracted light that bounced from precious metal to my brain. From that moment on, the rooms of my future were filling up with glass display cases in which I was mentally placing object after object.

Beside me the woman I had been following for months turned from this, laughing a little at a finger bone surrounded by a tiny silver Gothic cathedral. She looked in my eyes for her own and found material need instead. Still I took her hand, leading her down the centre aisle, through the main portal to the square. There she, not I, sang the obligatory praises of Donatello's Gattamelata, a man I considered too small for his magnificent horse, yet one of the few monuments I can still bring to mind as if I were standing before it right now.

By the time we reached Venice our parties were openly travelling together. No one, my tutor included, opposed the courtship any longer. He had promised, in fact, to speak to my father about the unimportance of choosing a wife with a title and the fine background of her particular family. We had won them all: she with her charm and I with my obstinacy. Then, within a few steps of my goal, the network of collecting threw its grid across my life. It was as simple as trading one obsession for another and as complicated as interlacing on a brooch. Almost imperceptibly the focus of my passion shifted. I began to finish all our discussions with definite, conclusive statements, tying all the strings of conversation into a final tidy knot. And there was nothing left to say. I began to speak of actual wonders in the city and then to immediately guide her to those wonders. And there was nothing left to anticipate. I read all the letters I received aloud in her presence, clearing up any vague details with absolute definitions. And there were no unanswered questions.

I DISCOVERED GLASS in Venice. My vision altered. The city itself seemed made of glass, reflecting from all that still water. At first I visited shop after shop with my companions, not yet wishing to be alone with it, my new treasure. I called it frozen liquid, captured gesture. After three days I set out by myself and crossed the lagunas by gondola, heading for Murano.

During my first visit I bought sixteen *lattimo* chocolate cups with sepia cathedrals painted on their bottoms, and a great quantity of blue glass – imitation lapis lazuli for the handles of my future tableware, tens of vases in clear pastel, thin lines like roads on a map all across their surfaces, transparent plates where enamel landscapes floated. In subsequent days I had crate after crate packed and shipped to London. I chose cups, phials, pitchers, saucers, goblets, and large chandeliers. And then some works of more fantastic nature: a ship complete with sails and riggings and a tree in full leaf. Finally, on my last day in Venice, I went in search of looking-glass and picked out five large mirrors surrounded by ornate glass frames.

On the last evening I walked with her in the low sun by one of those lengthy sheets of water. I stopped to pick up a pebble and dropped it casually to the spot where her slender reflection wavered, watching as her image shattered, simultaneously, in the water and in my mind. From then on she was clear glass and broken from me. I could not see her but to see through her to the monuments of the city; her left arm becoming a distant spire, her shoulder the ornamental corner of a palace. The phial of her body seemed fine-edged and thin. I knew then that I had imagined in her a glass so delicate and clear she had become all but invisible to me. I could not touch her but to break her.

When I returned from that city of heat and silence, London seemed noisy and cold. I quickly finalized the arrangements for the marriage my family approved of, one that would pave the way to my present dukedom. My wife and I are very fond of each other. There have been no other women in my life.

I continued to acquire glass, of course, returning to Venice again and again over the years, and to the rest of Italy, to look for older and finer pieces. Now my rooms are filled with objects so fragile, so delicate, that I can hardly bear to enter them, afraid that one careless movement, or even the slight wind caused by my passing, might bring about the destruction of the empire I've spent my life's energies acquiring. My blown glass obsessions. My delicate vocation.

And now, after sixty years, this final shift of attention. The rooms of my country house are full, my collection is complete. I have locked the door and walked away for the last time. Thousands of beautiful objects are in my possession, safe behind stronger glass, protected by walls of stone. And I don't want them, don't want the burden of them, the fear, the inability to cope with a strong wind or horses galloping by the window. I don't want them, want instead a memory – a young girl standing in the light, holding a tray filled with glasses of sherry. Want to be able to remember the words she spoke, the colour of her eyes.

I don't want the old man who stares back at me from those five dark mirrors. Even though not a single object in his entire collection has ever been damaged, his dreams are filled with broken glass and tears.

Hotel Verbano

SLOTH

HOTEL VERBANO floats on the still lake like a child's toy, like the model of an ocean liner under glass, like a pink cloud on the horizon. Occasionally it is just a shadow of itself, occasionally it is more precise than palaces.

Getting there. The *vaporetto* cuts the lake in half, gliding on a sharp keel. Behind me a crease like the life line on your palm. There is no wind, little noise, just the ticking of the small motor at the stern and the gentle lick of water at the prow. My arm drops over the side of the boat and my hand is touched by the soft warm lake.

Around me mountains alter their firm positions. Appearing, then opening up to reveal more mountains. Hotel Verbano increases in size. I recognize the features on the garden statues. I begin to identify flowers. Overhead, a sky of pure white, its surface uninterrupted by cloud formations or areas of blue. The lake, too – smooth, featureless. Tiny beads of moisture begin to cover my skin.

When I walk through the lobby of Hotel Verbano, my clean damp footprints remain on the marble floor. The key to my room jingles in my hand. Already I am very tired. Closing my eyes in the elevator, I see mountains moving. Firm and calm.

I never dream at Hotel Verbano. Sleep is neutral, day is dream. Looking from my balcony, I see guests adrift in rowboats, their long white skirts trailing in the water. Some toss their hair back, others sip pastel-coloured iced drinks. Their purple eyes are filled with moving mountains.

The first day. As I walk in the gardens the statues smile at me. They wear white peacocks as hats and bracelets, wreaths of flowers round their necks. I find I cannot remember their iconography, cannot recall their period, their history. Returning to the room, I sink into a mattress of soft white feathers. The walls are covered with sea shells drawn from an ocean far from here. Each one contains some echo from the sea. I hear its quiet breath before I sleep.

The second day, I walk around the circumference of the island that is this hotel. This is Verbano's rough edge. Here I stumble over boulders and my ankles are torn by the branches of fallen trees. I see a vague dark shape in the water, very close to my right foot, and I realize it is a drowned cat, partially concealed by water, moving back and forth with the subtle motions of the lake. Its white fur is beginning to peel and float away from its body. The small waves are a cradle to its long sleep, and the way it moves in them is a dance of decay.

In the dining-room the waiters walk on noiseless shoes, anticipate my order, and are never mistaken. I eat the soft fish of the lake and white bread. I add milk to my tea to destroy its colour. My wine is always white, like the table-cloth, the saucers, the ceiling over my head.

Once, after a lengthy sleep, I open the shutters and I see the moon rise over a wall of mountains. The white path it makes on the water is as still as ice, until an empty drifting boat intersects it and the black of the lake is broken into stars. I return to my bed and sleep on until noon.

Eventually the flowers in the dining-room, the urns on the terrace, the marble statues, the gravel garden paths are all covered by a light mist, as if my eyes cannot quite focus. The pale omelette on my plate, the glass in my hand lose texture, become unfamiliar, soft. A knife dissolves in my grasp. The muscles in my eyelids relax, my mouth begins to droop.

By the third day, the mist has turned to fog, eliminating mountains. I visit the ten terraces where even the dark cypress has become opaque. The abandoned bird machine stands silent – pale blue doves poised, their mechanical mouths open, miming song. Dusty olive trees shrink below me and mimosa closes at my touch. Past the camphor level sits the greenhouse, empty in this gentlest of seasons. A white sailboat floats, becalmed, almost invisible, halfway from the shore.

Again in my room, opening the windows for air, closing the shutters for dark, I look once more out to the lake. The seam of the horizon has vanished, leaving a closed circle of atmosphere. The cat floats by. The long train of fur and skin attached to its

left rear paw is about to separate forever. Guests adrift in rowboats sing indistinguishable lullabies. I turn towards the comfort of the bed.

The last thing that I notice is a thin white curtain floating on
the breeze that penetrates the shutters.

John's Cottage

SOMETIMES what you are running away from and what you find when you stop running and arrive somewhere else are almost the same thing – variations on a ghostly theme. Then, a subsequent experience can become a positive print of a shadowy negative in the mind. Understand. There were originally two Johns; a dark silhouette followed by an idea. The latter added detail, colour to the outline of the former. And then there was only one.

In the not too distant past each time I thought of the first John the flat human shape of Peter Pan's shadow leapt over the window sill of my imagination. Something about the way that shadow was folded up and placed inside a square object that may very well have been a drawer or toy box but that sticks in my mind as a suitcase. Folded up and placed inside some kind of luggage. You see, John's shadow was always in my luggage, and no matter how far I ran or where I ended up, that shadow ended up there too. Even if I was certain that I had left it at home.

Home. That place where John's shadow sometimes rang the phone but more often did not – the real John being busy in some office somewhere in another city. One stupid wire connecting our breathing, our tense silences; our bodies occupying rooms that were foreign to the other. Let me put it this way. I knew every detail of the rooms I lived in; the cracked paint around the windows, the stains on the carpets, that bit in the corner where the wallpaper was beginning to peel. I assume that John knew the peculiarities of his rooms as well. But neither of us knew anything about the other's house – about the place where the other really lived. That was the nature of our relationship.

I always liked the idea that Peter Pan slid across the window ledge and took over the air of Wendy's room. I liked his curiosity; the way he examined object after object so that, by the time he reached the very surprised Wendy, who was sitting bolt upright in her bed, he really knew her quite well; all about her window sashes and bedside tables, all about her music box and stuffed toys and sleeping brothers. He knew her well enough to demand that she sew his shadow back on immediately. Which she did, making everything more or less as it should be. John knew nothing of the interior of my rooms and didn't care to know as far as I could tell. So, as a result, I gained full possession of his shadow. He just never knew me well enough to ask for it back. Perhaps he wasn't even aware that I had it.

Once the shadow was back in place, back where it should be, Wendy and Peter began to have adventures. John and I shared no adventures. We met in neutral rooms in the neutral suburbs of what could have been any city in the world. It was all poured concrete and mirrors and plate-glass windows that looked out on more poured concrete. You couldn't take much home with you from spaces such as these. It would be unlikely that you would even remember the pattern on the spread or the pictures on the walls. Nobody stayed for long in these rooms and we knew it. They passed right through them on their way back to the unique furniture of their real lives. This was just the way John wanted it. The memory of me or anything to do with me was something he could do without. Because I was in love with him this angered and hurt me even though I knew that things could be no other way. Perhaps it was this hurt, this anger that made me unconsciously steal his shadow.

I was always running away from John one way or another: planes to here, planes to there, trains to places where there were no phones. Phones that ring, phones that remain silent, phones that are full of awkward sentences and tense silences. I was always running away to anonymous addresses in foreign countries. Sometimes I was annoyed to find John's shadow in my suitcase when I arrived; sometimes, however, I was relieved. A bit of familiarity in a strange place. And without the possibility of having to deal with the neutrality of the real John this could be comforting. The shadow, I felt, had the ability to care.

And it was portable – unlike John who stayed, stayed, stayed where he was. Stayed with his wife, stayed with his kids, stayed in the city. He wouldn't have followed me anywhere, not that John, not that real John. He made me come to him in those grey neutral rooms he rented. He locked me into them and pushed me out of them. He covered himself with me and then he showered me off. But I had his shadow with me later for some company.

More than anything, though, I missed knowing some other kind of rooms; rooms where something, anything, belonged to him, belonged to me, belonged to us.

THIS TIME when I arrived at the airport in northern England I was full of John, full of him. On the plane I had read books that I knew he liked, expressed to the stranger beside me opinions that I knew were his. I was even wearing a pair of jeans that were similar to his. Oh, I was full of him all right, more than I usually was when I was running away, and why? Because he had utterly rejected me before I had left. It was always like that: the greater the hurt, the more the compulsion to run away, the more he pumped through my blood stream and nervous system like some kind of bad drug leaving me weak with longing and self-loathing. His indifference was a stimulus to my obsession, it was as simple as that. And so, by the time I stepped off the plane in northern England I was so stunned, so absorbed that I wasn't sure that his shadow wasn't my own, that I hadn't sewn it onto the toes of the wrong body by mistake.

JOHN IN MY BLOODSTREAM, John in my nervous system and John's shadow attached to every other part of my body as I walked up the flagstone path towards the stone cottage I had rented. Beside me, oblivious to all but my material luggage, my new landlady, Mrs. Southam, who was discussing, at some length, the hardships of the present winter, hardships which had continued well into this month of March. Snow was still present on the tops of the distant hills and the windows of the house were fogged in a way that suggested to me that, although it might be warmer in than out, one would still be able to see one's breath in the parlour. (John's breath or mine?)

'You'll be wanting,' she was saying, 'coal, ... maybe smokeless like we're supposed to burn. But it's very dear and we burn the old stuff and never get caught. Stanley will make delivery down chute,' she added, thoughtfully.

'Stanley ...?'

'Me husband.'

Shades of John's wife slid into my imagination. I had never met her and had no idea what she was like. But I had invented her, over and over. A practical, attractive woman of the skirt and sweater variety – one who cooked wholesome meals or, if I was feeling tired, a snivelling neurotic with perpetual psychosomatic pains and the ability to manipulate through guilt.

When John travelled to other places, which wasn't very often, it was she who accompanied him and so, later, when he spoke about those rare times it would be she who shared his memories.

He shared nothing but poured concrete with me. Nothing but walls and windows with curtains obscuring views and doors which either locked you in or out.

THE COTTAGE WAS COLD and bright and clean and sharp; the way certain landscapes look in the sun after a sudden, fierce shower. Dustless, smokeless. Even the fire, when I lit it, had a polished look, not at all what you associate with flame, and appeared slightly ridiculous quivering away in the sunlight. But then, I came from a country where central heating abounds and where fires are lit for decorative purposes at night. I remembered that things always looked different to me in a warm room and I felt that this fire might change shape and colour as it began to throw out heat.

Then John's shadow nudged my elbow and suggested that I might want to write John a letter in which I could describe my new surroundings. But I knew that a letter from me was the last thing that John wanted to see slipping through the letter slot into the entrance hall of his real life, lying there on the welcome mat demanding an explanation for its presence. So I contented myself, instead, with taking the shadow on a tour of the place we were to inhabit for the next few months.

As it had been, in the beginning, a hand-loom weaver's cottage, a row of three light-giving windows dominated the single room on the first and second floors, providing all that sunlight that competed with the fire. Upstairs these windows reproduced themselves in sun squares on the lavender-coloured bedspread where I now flung my suitcase. As I unpacked I looked outside to the swells of the hills; moorgrass and then higher snow, and higher still, the uninterrupted blue of the sky. Suddenly, I remembered that there had been sky in some of the rooms I had entered with John, that occasionally, when the room had been on the tenth or eleventh floor he had felt safe enough to leave the curtains open and there had been all that blue behind gigantic sheets of plate glass. And once a bird of some sort had swung down from above and had hit the invisible barrier of the window with a thud that resembled the sound of a snowball hitting a car window. John had been very disturbed by that and had pulled the curtains so that no more birds would be fooled and harmed. So that they would know that the barrier existed and would always exist and would never change or go away. Because it made it different from all the other times, the sound of that bird breaking itself against our solid transparent window was the only real memory that John and I shared though neither one nor the other of us ever mentioned it. And sometimes I actually believed I could hear an echo of that noise when we were making love; as if it were love itself trying to get into the room, stunning itself on the invisible barrier and then falling ten stories to its death.

BY THE TIME Mr. Southam delivered the coal it had been dark for several hours. I had prepared and eaten my evening meal and the fire was looking warm and natural in the lamplight. Little decorative parts of the cottage that I hadn't noticed in the afternoon were beginning to attract my attention: a small Staffordshire piece, for instance, of a lady sitting on a horse with a man standing beside her, and a basket, shaped like a frog, with buttons, thread and a needle inside. There was also a round beaten-brass plate over the mantel with a scene depicting lots of good cheer in an old-fashioned pub. One of the men on the plate resembled John in the shape of his high forehead and the way he held his head before he lifted a glass to his lips. I was just thinking this when I heard the coal spilling into the cellar below. Seconds later both Southams presented themselves at my door and were enticed inside for a drink.

Mrs. Southam inquired about tea towels and can openers

while Mr. Southam settled back into one of the large comfortable arm chairs and lit his pipe. Although they spoke to me separately and rarely to each other there was an authority about their togetherness. You simply would never question it, even in a crowded room. I, who had never been married, was, for some reason, at that moment astonished by the irrefutable fact of it. I found myself addressing questions to both of them as if they were merely two sides of the same person.

'How long have you people owned the cottage?' I asked and 'Was it in need of many repairs?'

'Two or three years,' Mr. Southam answered. 'I put in window glass, fixed the door, replaced the stairs.'

'Stanley is a carpenter,' Mrs. Southam added with a certain amount of pride. 'He paints the walls too, after renters leave that have been here for a long time.'

A long time, I thought, John and I were never anywhere for a long time. If you added up all the hours we had spent together they probably wouldn't fill a week.

Mr. Southam knocked the bowl of his pipe against the edge of a thick glass ashtray making a little mountain there of burnt and unburnt tobacco.

'It were unsightly when I bought it, which is why it weren't dear. A lad lived there, like a gypsy, with nothing but the clothes on his back and what he grew out there.' He jerked his head towards the windows which looked out on a small garden. 'That and what he caught on t' moor.'

I imagined a barefoot boy, about fourteen, wearing a torn shirt and sporting a dagger in his teeth. One of Peter Pan's lost boys.

'Well, he were hardly a boy by the time he departed,' said Mrs. Southam speaking at last to her husband, 'he must have been near thirty year old.'

'Did he own the cottage?' I asked as my mind erased the image of the lost boy.

'Aye,' said Mrs. Southam, 'in that it were left to him by his Gran who he had lived with almost always as his parents had died. Old Mrs. Wetherald she kept the place right clean but after she died he let it open up.'

'Open up?' I asked.

'You know,' Mr. Southam explained, 'a window goes and you don't replace it with nothing but cardboard. Roof tiles blow away in the wind. It's a hazard around here, the wind.'

As they were leaving Mrs. Southam asked me if I would like a pint or two of milk delivered to the door and because I found the idea quaint I said that I would.

'I'll just tell the milkman, then, to come around and speak to you,' she continued, 'I'll just tell him there's someone wanting milk up to John's cottage.'

I was speechless with shock and astonishment and my surprise must have shown in my face.

'That were his name,' she said, 'the lad who owned the house. Everyone in the village still calls this John's cottage.'

THAT FIRST NIGHT, although it was still clear, the wind picked up and started fooling around with everything that wasn't nailed down and several things that were. I could hear the empty garbage tins bumping against the wooden box that Mr. Southam had built to hold them and all of the window panes rattling in their sashes. I could also hear the kitchen door downstairs creaking slightly on its hinges because this was a wind that knew how to get inside despite the efforts of an excellent carpenter like Mr. Southam to keep it out. The letter slot was clattering away with a rhythm that was almost musical and I thought about how John's letter slot would never feel the caress of words from me and how this one would hear nothing from him either, and I wondered what letters, if any, had come through the slot for that other John, that wild John who had owned the cottage.

I lay upstairs in the lavender bed with all the lights out and the curtains open. Where there had been three panels of sunlight earlier in the day there were now three panels of moonlight and, although I couldn't see the moon from where I lay, it was doing a great job of brightening the room. Getting in everywhere with the same persistence as the wind. I stayed awake for so long, not unhappily, that I actually watched those panels move across the bed. I felt warm and safe, despite all the wild activity around me and eventually, after a few hours, I fell asleep.

I was awakened at about three o'clock by an even more furious wind and an even louder banging, this time coming from the little attic room on the third floor and I knew something had broken loose up there and that I would have to investigate if I was to get any more sleep that night. As I climbed the narrow staircase I remembered from childhood all the things that could possibly sneak into your bedroom at night; Peter Pan and Tinkerbell and Santa Claus and the Tooth Fairy and Guardian Angels and The Lord to take your soul if you happened to die before you woke and I decided that the moon and the wind should be added to this list of benevolent intruders.

Although there were no windows in the tiny attic room it was, if possible, even more filled with moonlight than the bedroom below and much more filled with wind. The source of both these elements, and of the banging noise, was a small skylight whose latch, for some reason, was not fastened. As I reached up to secure the mechanism I looked directly into the face of the moon which was framed, dead centre, in the single pane of glass. It was a male face; startling and powerful. John, I thought, sadly resigned to my obsession. But no, it wasn't the face I was running away from, or even the face of the shadow I'd brought with me. It was some other face. The face of a stranger – a special stranger. A face filled with all the oddly familiar unfamiliarity of someone you are going to get to know very well, very soon.

I SPENT the next few days exploring the village and everywhere I went people spoke to me about the cottage and about the strange John who had lived there. He was evidently a great favourite and everyone became kind and friendly the moment they discovered where I was staying. 'John's cottage,' they said over and over, smiling, leaning on garden walls, standing behind counters, sitting on stools in the pub, until, after a few encounters I would announce proudly, 'I'm living in John's cottage,' and wait for the positive response. 'Ah, John,' the men would say, 'he were a good mate.' 'That John,' the women would add, 'that rascal.' And in their voices there was a memory of a benevolent teaser; a memory of proximity and warmth.

By the third day the cottage was warm all the time. I had learned the fire: how to build it and restructure it, how to move it around in the little theatre of its hearth. How to make it leap up or fold down into glowing coals that both kept and gave away heat all night long. I knew how to construct that gentle slope that meant that when I returned after four hours in the pub in the evening it would still be strong and how to construct that steeper slope that would guarantee that after nine hours of sleep I would descend the stairs into comfort. Even though the wind shrieked all night long and crept in through every crack it could.

Those early mornings, though, I usually awoke to the shadow, and with a start, as if it had dreamed all night beside me, wakened sooner than I and then dug its elbow into my ribs. Especially on those still, cloudy days when neither wind nor sun demanded entrance to the cottage. Then I would lie flat on the bed for some time and struggle, almost physically, with some of the things that John had said to me before I left. 'You should get married and have children,' he said, or 'I can't just change my life for you.' These statements followed by long silences and me adrift in a sea of pain. Remembering sentences like these in the cottage I would be attacked by a feeling of vertigo so intense the bed would be like Peter Pan's conquered pirate ship careering through the sky.

But then I would dig my hands into the flesh of the mattress and force myself up and out and onto the floor. Then downstairs to the reliable fire – its warmth, its comfort.

ON FRIDAY NIGHTS everyone in the village over the age of sixteen came to the pub to talk about animals and unemployment, births, deaths and current events. When they discussed weather, which in that riding was difficult to avoid, they talked about it in terms of its absence indoors. 'There is no rain in here,' they would say as they entered through the door and began to remove their dripping outer garments, or 'there's no ice over there by the fire.'

'John let the rain in,' one of them might say to me knowing by now that my interest was acute – didn't I live in his cottage? 'When the roof tiles blew away he just let them blow. Mind the time,' this narrator would continue, turning to include his neighbour on the other side of the bench, 'that river came right down the stairs and another one in the kitchen door at the back and out by the door at the front.'

'Moor foxes,' one of the women told me, 'scampered in and out of the cottage like small children, and birds nested right on the kitchen shelves.'

'Moles,' an elderly farmer announced,' burrowing up between the flags near the fire.'

'John would have regular waterfalls coming down the stairs and never mind a bit.'

'And what about the fire?' I asked, curious because of my own recent mastery of same.

'Oh, John always had a good fire and a good pot beside it full of strong tea. He was right comfortable there, was John.'

Yes, I thought, he would be. Did Snow White lack for comfort when she lived in the cottage with the Seven Dwarfs? – which, if I remember my Disney movies, was full of turquoise birds and baby deer and rabbits of all sizes and lantern-carrying dwarfs scurrying in and out of the doors. Poor Snow White. She wasn't very comfortable anywhere else; not in her stepmother's castle, not in her glass catafalque, not in whatever place her awakening prince lugged her off to. But there in that disordered cottage she glowed to such an extent that you were certain that comfort was the rule she lived by. And how comfortable Wendy appeared to be in her night nursery with its wide open windows, its flying boys, its fairies, its dog nanny! She may have been occasionally surprised but she was certainly never ill at ease.

'What happened to John?' I wanted to know. I asked this question several times during my evenings at the pub. 'Oh,' they invariably answered vaguely, and without sadness, 'he sold the cottage and moved away. He were a good lad, were John.'

A good lad who was becoming, for me, as unreal and as real as a memorized fairy tale.

I WALKED during the day either up to the higher moorlands where snow still shone or down into the valley below the cottage where the first flowers of spring were beginning to appear. It was a choice between two seasons and a choice also between openness and enclosure. But it wasn't long before I realized that although the winds were not as strong in the valley the sense of enclosure wasn't as strong either as one might expect in contrast to the sweep of the moors. The difference was in the details of the place – the crumbling walls, the becks, the wooden bridges, the trees, which were noticeably absent on higher ground. The moors were composed of great swaths of ling, heather and bilberry and the colours there were earthy charcoals, sepias and umbers. The valley was a deep, lush green.

Whether I sauntered down from above or climbed up from below, when I returned I always dug for a while in John's garden. Once I unearthed the arm of a china doll, unbroken, with its little hand curved into a shape like a bowl. Although this small object could never have been part of anything that belonged to the cottage's John I kept it with me always as a reminder of him and what he was beginning to represent to me.

Oh banisher of shadows, oh heart like a cup, filling.

ONE DAY when I'd wandered farther than usual down the length of the valley I came across a bit of architecture that I decided was the very essence of John – the new John, the one I was getting to know. There he stood, constructed of strong millstone grit, surrounded by tangled clouds of what would become, in summer, wild roses. A pure stream of water ran straight through the middle of him carrying trout, those bright-eyed beauties of fresh water. Birds drank there. Some bathed. Sun and wind dominated for the roof had been gone for a long time. Below all that sky row after row of glassless windows – the true wind-holes of old, which if you stood outside the walls allowed you to see the confused garden of the interior, or if you climbed through them into that garden, gave you clear views of the rest of the world.

After that it wasn't long before the idea of *John of the Open Windows,* as I began to call him, stepped in through his open cottage door and, of course, I welcomed him as I would welcome the returning spirit of any house. The shadow of *John of the Neutral Rooms* was preparing to leave me anyway, unable as he was to live in open spaces.

Everywhere there is weather now, it colours all the rooms as the idea and I sleep in the lavender bed. And then there are the elements that belong to us; song of wind, tint of moonlight until morning. The reliable fire. Then birdsong, the bright eyes of a wild animal gaining entrance to your life and wind breathing spring up to the higher moorlands.

Italian Postcards

WHENEVER SHE IS SICK, home from school, Clara the child is allowed to examine her mother's Italian postcards, a large pile of them, which are normally bound with a thick leather band and kept in a bureau drawer. Years later when she touches postcards she will be amazed that her hands are so large. Perhaps she feels that the hands of a child are proportionally correct to rest like book ends on either side of landscapes. Or maybe it's not that complicated; maybe she just feels that, as an adult, she can't really see these colours, those vistas, and so, in the odd moments when she does, she must necessarily be a child again.

The room she lies in on weekdays, when she has managed to stay home from school, is all hers. She'll probably carry it around with her for the rest of her life. Soft grey wallpaper with sprays of pink apple blossom. Pink dressing table (under the skirts of which her dolls hide, resting on their little toy beds), cretonne curtains swathed over a window at the foot of the bed she occupies, two or three pink pillows propping her up. Outside the window a small back garden and some winter city or another. It doesn't really matter which.

And then the postcards; turquoise, fuchsia, lime green — improbable colours placed all over the white spread and her little hands picking up one, then another, as she tries to imagine her mother walking through such passionate surroundings.

In time, her mother appears at the side of the bed. Earlier in the morning she brought the collection of postcards. Now she holds a concoction of mustard and water wrapped in white flannel and starts to undo the little buttons on the little pyjama top.

WHILE THE MUSTARD PLASTER burns into her breastbone Clara continues to look at the postcards. Such flowers, such skies, such suns burning down on such perfect seas. Her mother speaks the names of foreign towns; *Sorrento,* she says, *Capri, Fiesole, Garda, Como,* and then after a thoughtful pause,

You should see Como. But most of all you should see Pompeii.

Clara always saves Pompeii, however, until the end, until after her mother has removed the agonizing poultice and has left the room – until after she has gone down the stairs and has resumed her orderly activities in the kitchen. Then the child allows the volcano to erupt, to spill molten lava all over the suburban villas, the naughty frescos, the religious mosaics. And all over the inhabitants of the unsuspecting ancient town.

IN THE POSTCARDS Pompeii is represented, horrifyingly, fascinatingly, by the inhabitants themselves, frozen in such attitudes of absolute terror or complete despair that they teach the child everything she needs to know about heartbreak and disaster: how some will put their arms up in front of their faces to try to ward it off, how others will resign themselves, sadly, to its strength. What she doesn't understand is how such heat can freeze, make permanent, the moment of intensest pain. A scream in stone that once was liquid. What would happen, she wonders, to these figures if the volcano were to erupt again? How permanent are they?

And she wonders about the archaeologists who have removed the stone bodies from the earth and, without disturbing a single gesture, have placed them in glass display cases inside the museum where they seem to float in the air of their own misfortune ... clear now, the atmosphere empty of volcanic ash, the glass polished.

These are the only postcards of Pompeii that Clara's mother has. No bright frescos, no recently excavated villas, no mosaics; only these clear cases full of grey statues made from what was once burning flesh.

TWENTY-FIVE YEARS LATER when Clara stands with her husband at the entrance to Hotel Oasie in Assisi she has seen Sorrento, Como, Capri and has avoided Pompeii altogether.

'Why not?' her husband asks.

'Nobody lives there,' she replies.

But people live here, in this Tuscan hill town; the sun has burned life into their faces. And the colours in the postcards were real after all – they spill out from red walls into the vegetable displays on the street, they flash by on the backs of over-dressed children. Near the desk of the hotel they shout out from travel posters. But in this space there is no sun; halls of cool remote marble, sparse furnishings, and, it would seem, no guests but themselves.

'Dinner,' the man behind the desk informs them, 'between seven and nine in the big salon.'

Then he leads them, through arched halls, to their room.

Clara watches the thick short back of the Italian as she walks behind him, realizing as she does that it is impossible to imag-ine muscle tone when it is covered by smooth black cloth. She looks at the back of his squarish head. Cumbersome words such as *basilica, portcullis, Etruscan* and *Vesuvius* rumble dis-turbingly, and for no apparent reason, through her mind.

Once the door has clicked behind them and the echoing footsteps of the desk clerk have disappeared from the outside hall, her husband examines the two narrow beds with displea-sure and shrugs.

'Perhaps we'll find a way,' he says, 'marble floors are cold.' Then looking down, 'Don't think these small rugs will help much.'

Then, before she can reply, they are both distracted by the view outside the windows. Endless olive groves and vineyards and a small cemetery perched halfway up the hill. Later in the evening, after they have eaten pasta and drunk rough, red wine in the enormous empty dining room, they will see little twin-kling lights shine up from this spot, like a handful of stars on the hillside. Until that moment it will never have occurred to either of them that anyone would want to light a tomb at night.

> *Go and light a tomb at night*
> *Get with child a mandrake root.*

Clara is thinking Blake ... in Italy of all places, wandering through the empty halls of Hotel Oasie, secretly inspecting rooms. All the same so far; narrow cots, tiny rugs, views of vineyards and the graveyard, olive trees. Plain green walls. These rooms, she thinks, as Blake evaporates from her mind, these rooms could use the services of Mr. Domado's Wallpaper Company, a company with one employee – the very unhappy Mr. Domado himself. He papered her room once when she was a sick child and he was sick with longing for his native land. When Italian postcards coincidentally littered her bedspread like fallen leaves. *Ah, yes,* said Mr. Domado, sadly picking up one village and then another. *Ah, yes.*

And he could sing ... Italian songs. Arias that sounded as mournful as some of the lonelier villages looked. Long, long sobbing notes trembling in the winter sunshine, while she lay propped on pink pillows and her mother crept around in the kitchen below silently preparing mustard plasters. Mr. Domado, with tears in his voice, eliminating spray after spray of pink apple blossoms, replacing them with rigid geometric designs, while Clara studied the open mouths of the stone Pompeii figures and wondered whether, at the moment of their death, they were praying out loud. Or whether they were simply screaming.

Screaming, she thinks now, as she opens door after door of Hotel Oasie, would be practically a catastrophe in these echoing marble halls. One scream might go on for hours, as her footsteps seem to every time she moves twenty feet or so down to the next door, as the click of the latch seems to every time she has closed whatever door she has been opening. The doors are definitely an addition to the old, old building and appear to be pulled by some new longitudinal force back into the closed position after her fingers release their cold, steel knobs. Until she opens the door labelled *Sala Beatico Angelico* after which no hotel room will ever be the same.

NEITHER CLARA nor her husband speak Italian, so to ask for a complete explanation would be impossible.

'A Baroque church!' she tells him later. 'Not a chapel but a complete church. All the doors are the same, *this* door is the same except for the words on it, and you open it and there, instead of a hotel room, is a complete church.'

'It appears,' he says after several moments of reflection, 'that we have somehow checked into a monastery.'

SURE ENOUGH, when she takes herself out to the rose garden later in the afternoon to sit in the sun and to read *The Little Flowers of Santa Chiara* in preparation for the next day's trip to the basilica, the hotel clerk greets her, dressed now in a clerical collar. Clara shows no surprise, as if she had known all along that hers was not to be a secular vacation; as if the idea of a retreat had been in her mind when she planned the trip. She shifts the book a little so that the monastic gardener will notice that she is reading about St. Francis's holy female friend. He, however, is busy with roses; his own little flowers, and though he faces her while he works his glance never once meets hers. She is able, therefore, to observe him quite closely ... the dark tan of his face over the white of his collar, his hands, which move carefully but easily through the roses, avoiding thorns. Clara tries, but utterly fails, to imagine the thoughts of a priest working in a rose garden. Are they concerned, as they should be, with *God* ... the thorns, perhaps, signifying a crown, the dark red stain of the flower turning in his mind to the blood of Christ? Or does he think only of roses and their health ... methods of removing the insect from the leaf ... the worm from the centre of the scarlet bud? His face gives her no clue; neither that nor the curve of his back as he stoops to remove yet another vagrant weed from the soft brown earth surrounding the bushes.

Clara turns again to her book, examining the table of contents; 'The Circle of Ashes', 'The Face in the Well', 'The Hostage of Heaven', 'The Bread of Angels', 'The Meal in the Woods', and finally, at the bottom of the list, 'The Retinue of Virgins.' St. Francis, she discovers, had never wanted to see Chiara. The little stories made this perfectly clear. Sentence after sentence described his aversion. After he had clothed her in sackcloth and cut off all her hair in the dark of the Italian night, after he had set her on the path of poverty and had left her with her sisters at St. Damien's, after she had turned into a *hostage of heaven* and had given up eating all together, Francis withdrew. *Beware of the poison of familiarity with women,* he had told his fellow friars. In a chapter entitled 'The Roses', the book stated that Francis had wanted to place an entire season between himself and Chiara. *We will meet again when the roses bloom,* he had said, standing with his bare feet in the snow. Then God had decided to make the roses bloom spontaneously, right there, right then, in the middle of winter.

Clara cannot decide, now, what possible difference that would make. As a matter of fact, it looks to her as if God were merely playing a trick on Chiara and Francis. If Francis said they would meet again when the roses bloom, why not have the roses bloom right now? Perhaps then there would be no subsequent meeting since the roses had already bloomed. This would have certainly been a puzzle for Chiara to work on during the dreary winter days that stretched ahead of her in the unheated convent. She could have worked it over and over in her mind like a rosary. It might have kept her, in some ways, very busy.

Francis, on the other hand, was always very busy. As the book said: *Francis came and went freely from St. Mary of the Angels but Chiara found herself like a prisoner at St. Damien's.* Francis might have dropped by to see Chiara while he was out rushing around, but he didn't. *On the other hand, Francis stayed well away from St. Damien's,* the book continued, *for he did not wish the common people should take scandal from seeing him going in and out.* So basically, it would appear that poor Chiara, poison that she was, rarely spoke to her mentor; the man whose principles she built her life around. At least not until 'The Meal in the Woods.'

After she had asked him repeatedly to share a meal with her, Francis finally relented. Speaking, once again to his fellow friars (he seemed never to have spoken to Chiara), he argued, *She has been a long time at St. Damien's. She will be happy to come out for a little while and to see in the daytime that place to which she first came at night, where her hair was cut from her, and where she was received among us. In the name of Jesus Christ we will picnic in the woods.* Somehow, during the course of this unusual picnic, the woods began to glow as if they were on fire. It is not clear to Clara whether God or Francis was responsible for this miracle. It may have been a collaboration. It is perfectly clear, however, that Chiara had nothing to do with it. Her role was that of appreciator – one that she, no doubt, played very well. And, as usual, she wasn't eating. The chapter ends with this statement: *Finally Chiara and Francis rose from the ground, overjoyed and filled with spiritual nourishment, not having touched as much as a crumb of the food.*

Clara is beginning to feel hungry. Delicious smells are coming from what she now knows is the refectory. The gardener is placing his tools, one by one, in the wheelbarrow. Then, without looking in her direction, he pushes the little vehicle away from her, towards the potting shed.

'OUR HOTEL CLERK,' she informs her husband at dinner, 'is a gardener as well as a priest. I was reading up on my namesake out on the terrace and I saw him in the garden, working away.'

'I discovered the other part of the building,' her husband replies. 'There is a glass door with *Keep Out* written on it in four languages, and then an entire wing where the priests must stay when they open the place to tourists.'

'You didn't peek?' asks Clara, fully aware that, had she discovered it, she might have opened the door.

'No ... written rules you know,' and then, 'Have you decided to like your namesake? Do you think you take after her?'

Clara reflects for a while. 'I think she was a very unhappy woman. She kept on wanting to see Francis and he kept not wanting to see her.'

'Probably just propriety, don't you think? You can't have Saint Francis spending a lot of time hanging around the convent you know, wouldn't look good.'

'Possibly ... but maybe it was just an excuse. Maybe he really *didn't* want to see her. The poor girl ... she was in love with him, I expect. He was probably God to her.'

'Maybe *he* was in love with *her* ... did that ever occur to you? Maybe that's why he stayed away.' Her husband glances to the end of the room. 'Look who's coming,' he says. 'Our desk clerk is not only a gardener and a priest, he is also a waiter.'

THE NEXT AFTERNOON Clara decides she will not visit the basilica after all. She would rather read in the rose garden than gaze at frescos.

'Later,' she tells her husband. 'You check it out, tell me about it.'

Postcard views and skies are outside the walls of the hotel as usual, and now the closer, more exaggerated colours of the roses. It is hotter than the previous day so the priest has abandoned his collar. Clara notices that he has a perfect mole situated right in the centre of his throat. A sort of natural stigmata, she decides.

The chapter entitled 'The Door of the Dead' fascinates her. She is reading it for the fourth time. It seems that the ancient houses in Assisi often had two doors; a large one through which the family normally came and went, and a smaller one, elevated above the ground, through which the dead were passed, feet first in their coffins. Chiara, on the night she went to meet Francis in the woods, decided to leave the house through the second door. *She wanted to get away secretly,* the book states, *and she was absolutely sure she would meet no one on the threshold of that door.* With the help of a minor miracle on God's part she was able to slide bolts and move hinges that had been rusted in position for fifteen years. Then she jumped lightly to the ground and ran out of the village. *Never again would she be able to return to her family,* the chapter concludes, *Chiara was dead. Chiara was lost. Chiara had passed over into another life.*

Clara wonders if the priest, who is working directly in front of her, has also passed over into another life, and whether, if this is so, the roses look redder to him than they do to her. Whether he lives a sort of *Through the Looking Glass* existence.

She adjusts the angle of her chair. He is working close enough now that their shadows almost touch. A vague sadness stirs near Clara's heart, stops, then moves again. Restless lava shifting somewhere in the centre of a mountain.

HER HUSBAND has decided that they will stay at Hotel Oasie for the remainder of their vacation. He likes it there. He likes Assisi. He is moved by all of it; as much, he says, by the electrified confessionals in the basilica as by the Giottos. He claims that the former are like the washrooms on a jumbo jet in that they have automatic *occupied* and *vacant* signs that are lighted from behind. He is amazed, he continues, at how easily the Italians have adapted their highly superstitious religion to modern technology ... the lighted tombs, the electric candles in front of religious statues, the *occupied* signs. This amuses and pleases him. He will write a sociological paper on it when they return to North America.

She isn't listening to him very carefully because she has fallen in love, just like that, bang, with the gardener, waiter, desk clerk, priest. She has, by now, spent four long afternoons with him in the rose garden and he has never once looked her way. Unless, she speculates, he looks her way when she is absorbed in *The Little Flowers of Santa Chiara*, which is possible. On the third afternoon she made up a little rule for herself that she would not lift her eyes from the book until a chapter was completely finished. In that way she has balanced her activities. Ten minutes of reading followed by ten minutes of studying the priest. This means, of course, that he is never in the same location after she finishes reading 'The Door of the Dead' as he was after she finished reading, say, 'A Kiss For the Servant.' She is then forced to look around for him which makes the activity more intriguing. One afternoon, after finishing the chapter called 'Infirmity and Suffering', she looked up and around and discovered that he had disappeared completely, simply slipped away while she was reading. Almost every other time, though, she is able to watch him collect his tools, place them in the wheelbarrow and walk towards the potting shed. And this makes her grieve a little, as one often does when a lengthy ritual has been appropriately completed.

'DID YOU KNOW,' she asks her husband angrily at dinner, 'Did you know that he wouldn't even let her come to see him when he was *dying*? I mean, isn't that taking it a bit too far? The man was dying and she asked if she could see him and he said no ... not until I'm *dead*.'

The priestly waiter serves the pasta. Clara watches his brown left hand approach the table and withdraw. '*Scusi*', he says as he places the dish in front of her. She cannot accuse him of never speaking to her. He has said *Scusi* in her presence now a total of seventeen times and once, when a meal was over, he looked directly into her eyes and had asked, 'You feeneesh?'

Now she stabs her fork deliberately into the flesh of the ravioli. 'Moreover,' she continues, 'that little book I am reading has next to nothing to do with Chiara ... mostly it's about Francis ... until he dies, of course ... then it's about her dying.' Forgetting to chew, Clara swallows the piece of pasta whole.

'Well,' says her husband, 'at least Giotto included her in some of the frescos.'

'Hmm,' she replies, unimpressed.

Clara gazes at the priest and her heart turns soft. He is staring absently into space. Imagining miracles, she decides, waiting out the dinner hour so that he can return to his quiet activities. Evening mass, midnight mass. Lighting candles, saying prayers. Does he make them up or follow rituals? Are there beads involved? Does he kneel before male or female saints? Any of this information would be important to her. Still, she would never dare enter the church she has discovered at the end of the hall. In fact, with the exception of the basilica with its electrified confessionals and famous frescos, she has not dared to open the door of any church in town. They are spaces that are closed to her and she knows it.

'Have you ever felt that a church was closed to you?' she asks her husband.

'Of course not,' he answers. 'After all, they are not only religious institutions ... they are great public monuments, great works of art. They are open to all of us.'

Clara sighs and turns her eyes, once again, to the priest. The way he is carrying the crockery back to the kitchen, as if it were a collection of religious artifacts he has recently blessed, almost breaks her heart.

IT IS HER FIFTH afternoon in the rose garden. He is there too, of course, pinning roses onto stakes. 'Crucifying them perhaps,' she thinks vaguely, lovingly.

By now she knows that this man will never *ever* respond to her, never *ever* speak to her; not in his language or hers – except at meal time when it is absolutely necessary. Because of this, the sadness of this, she loves him even harder. It is this continuous rejection that sets him apart. Rejection without object, without malice, a kind of healing rejection; one that causes a cleansing ache.

The ache washes over her now as she watches him stand back to survey his labours. She loves the way he just stands there looking, completely ignoring her. She is of absolutely no consequence in the story of his life, none whatsoever, and she loves him for this. She has no desire for change; no mediaeval fantasies about being the rose that he fumbles with, the saint that he prays to. She wants him just as he is, oblivious to her, causing her to ache, causing her to understand the true dimensions of hopelessness, how they are infinite.

She turns to the chapter in the book called 'The Papal Bull.' This is an oddly political section and her least favourite. It concerns the legitimization of the various Franciscan orders including Santa Chiara's Poor Sisters; the legitimization of lives of chosen self-denial. At this point Clara is finding it difficult to concentrate on what the Pope had to say, finds it difficult to care whether it was legitimate or not.

She is surprised, when she allows herself to look up, to find the priest's gaze aimed in her direction. She prepares to be embarrassed until she realized that he is, at last, reading the title of her book.

'SHE WANTED WORDS from him,' Clara tells her husband later. 'Words, you know, spiritual advice. You know what she got instead?'

'What?'

'She got a circle of ashes ... a circle of goddamn ashes! The book tries to make this seem profound ... the usual, he put a circle of ashes on the convent floor to demonstrate that all humans were merely dust or some such nonsense. You know what I think it meant? I think it meant that regardless of what Chiara wanted from him, regardless of how bad she might have wanted it, regardless of whether or not she ever swallowed a single morsel of food, or wore hair shirts, or humiliated herself in any number of ways, regardless of what she did, all she was *ever* going to get from him was a circle of ashes. I think it meant that she was entirely powerless and he was going to make damn certain that she stayed that way.'

'Quite a theory. I doubt the church would approve.'

'God, how she must have suffered!'

'Well,' he replies, 'wasn't that what she was supposed to do?'

IN THE MIDDLE of her seventh afternoon in the rose garden, after she has finished reading a chapter entitled 'The Canticle of the Creatures' (which she practically knows now by heart), and while she is studying the gestures of the priest who has moved from roses to vegetables, Clara decides that her heart is permanently broken. How long, she wonders, has it been this way? And why did it take this priest, this silent man who thinks and prays in a foreign language, to point it out to her? This is not a new disease, she knows suddenly. It's been there for a long, long time; a handicap she had managed to live with somehow, by completely ignoring it. How strange. Not to feel that pain that is always there, by never identifying it, never naming it. Now she examines the wound and it burns in the centre of her chest the way her mother's mustard plasters used to, the way molten lava must have in the middle of Vesuvius. Her broken heart has burned inside her for so long she assumed it was normal. Now the pain of it moves into her whole body; past the pulse at her wrists, down the fronts of her thighs, up into her throat. Then it moves from there out into the landscape she can see from the garden, covering all of it, every detail; each grey, green olive leaf, each electric candle in front of each small pathetic tomb, every bird, all of the churches she can never enter, poppies shouting in a distant field, this terrible swath of blue sky overhead, the few pebbles that cover the small area of terrace at her feet. And all the air that moves up and down her throat until she is literally gasping in pain.

Pure eruption. Shards of her broken heart are everywhere, moving through her bloodstream, lacerating her internally on their voyage from the inside out into the landscape, until every sense is raw. She can actually see the sound waves that are moving in front of her. She wonders if she has begun to shout but then gradually, gradually isolated sound dissolves into meaning as her brain begins its voyage back into the inside of her skull.

'Meesus,' the priest is saying, pointing to her book. 'She is still here, Santa Chiara. You go see her ... you go to Chiesa Santa Chiara ... you go there and you see her.'

Then he collects his gardening tools, places them in his wheelbarrow, and walks purposefully away.

SHE GOES ALONE, of course, two days later when she feels better and when she knows for sure they will be leaving Assisi the following morning. She is no longer in love with the priest; he has become what he always was, a small brown Italian busy with kitchen, clerical and gardening tools. The heartbreak, however, which preceded and will follow him is still with her, recognized now and accepted as she stands across the road from the Church of Santa Chiara watching a small cat walk on top of its shadow in the noonday sun.

Inside the door total darkness for a while, followed by a gradual adjustment of the eyes to dark inscrutable paintings and draped altars and the slow movements of two nuns who are walking towards the front of the church. She follows them, unsure now how to make her request and then, suddenly, the request is unnecessary. There, boom, illuminated by the ever present electricity, is the saint, laid out for all to see in her glass coffin. 'She is, you see,' one of the nuns explains, 'incorruptible. She is here seven hundred years and she does not decay because she is holy.'

Clara moves closer to see the dead woman's face, now glowing under the harsh twentieth-century light, and there, as she expects, is the pain. Frozen on Chiara's face the terrifying, wonderful pain; permanent, incorruptible, unable to decay. The dead mouth is open, shouting pain silently up to the electricity, past the glass, into the empty cave of the church, out into the landscape, up the street to the basilica where images of the live Chiara appear, deceitfully serene, in the frescos. It is the heartbreak that is durable, Clara thinks to herself, experiencing the shock of total recognition. Everything else will fade away. No wonder the saint didn't decay. A flutter of something sharp and cutting in Clara's own bloodstream and then she turns away.

Before she steps out into the street again she buys a postcard from one of the nuns. Santa Chiara in her glass coffin, as permanent as a figure from Pompeii in her unending, incorruptible anguish.

Clara places the card in an inside pocket of her handbag. There it will stay through the long plane ride home while her husband makes jokes about the washrooms resembling Italian confessionals. It will stay there and she will clutch the leather close to her broken heart; clutch the image of the dead woman's mouth. The permanent pain that moves past the postcard booth into the colours of the Italian landscape.